A FEW WORDS OF THANKS

Thanks to everyone who helped me make this book great. Thanks especially to:

Editor Katharine D'Souza
Wedding planner Janet Eboh-Sampson of Lotus Event Management
Lawyer Katherine Evans
Ali AElsey
Andy Conway
Carolyn Stubbs
Chris Hills
David Massey
David Wake
Dawn Abigail
Dennis Zaslona
Garry Hyde
Greg Howl
Helen Combe
Jeremy White
Jo Ullah
Karen Johnson
Laura Jane Gallagher
Michelle Armitage
Najum Qureshi
Nigel Howl
Patricia Gregory
Paula Good
Pete Crawford
Suzanne Ferris
Tiffany Elliott
Tim Kindberg

I really appreciate your help!

A.A. Abbott

BY A.A. ABBOTT

Up In Smoke

After The Interview

The Bride's Trail

The Vodka Trail

The Grass Trail

The Revenge Trail

*See **aaabbott.co.uk** for my blog, free short stories and more.
Sign up for my newsletter to receive news, freebies and offers.*

*Follow me on Twitter **@AAAbbottStories** and **Facebook**.*

THE REVENGE TRAIL

by A.A. Abbott

A.A. Abbott

Published by Perfect City Press.

This book was written by a British writer in British English.

ISBN 978-0-9929621-8-0

Contents

Chapter 1.   Marty

Marty Bridges' head pounded in time with the thumps on his office door. Whisking his wife to Paris for her birthday weekend had been fun, but had left him with a credit card bill and a hangover.

"Come in," he shouted, hardly voicing the words before his son burst into the office.

"Dad, we're in big trouble." Dan had visibly paled beneath his summer tan.

"What ails you, son? Sit down." Marty gestured to a meeting chair.

Dan remained standing. "I've rejected the latest shipment of Snow Mountain vodka."

Marty gawped. "You're joking. On what grounds?"

"We took delivery this morning," Dan said. "A hundred cases. The rest of the shipment is still in bond. I tested a bottle."

The procedure was usually a formality, leaving most of the bottle for the staff to sip or Dan to take home afterwards. "Go on," Marty said.

"There was methanol in it," Dan said.

"That's not good." Marty shook his head in disbelief. The pain in his temples intensified.

Drinkers could go blind, or even die, if they ingested methanol. It was a by-product of the distillation process, produced right at the start. A half-competent chemical engineer would drain it away before collecting and bottling the vodka. Had Marty sold any of this consignment, he'd have been ruined.

"Obviously, I just put it through the refractometer. I didn't go as far as drinking any." Dan ran his fingers through his untidy fair hair. He looked much as Marty had in his early thirties.

It was no wonder most of Marty's own locks had disappeared. "How could it happen? Don't tell me – Marina Aliyeva has sent the distillery to hell in a handbasket."

Marty had been wary of Marina even before she'd inherited the distillery in Bazakistan from her late, unlamented husband.

Dan shrugged, raising his eyes to the ceiling. "I guess so. I can't say. All I know is, I've been here for fifteen years, and every shipment's been clean as a whistle until now."

"And in the ten years before that."

Marty had imported Snow Mountain since the very first batch emerged from the production line. Purity and quality had been exceptional when the plant was run by Harry Aliyev and his predecessor, Sasha Belov. They were both skilled engineers and vodka enthusiasts. Each had also been married to, and outlived by, Marina.

She'd definitely had a hand in Belov's death, and possibly Aliyev's too. Harry Aliyev's illegitimate children thought so. They'd been denied a share in the distillery under Bazaki intestacy laws that gave the dead man's assets to his widow.

Marty shuddered, remembering the foxgloves, laburnum trees and oleander in Marina's garden. Those were just the poisonous plants he recognised. Harry Aliyev had supposedly died of natural causes: a heart attack, whilst in his mistress's embrace. It wouldn't have been beyond Marina's wit, or desire, to have helped her husband on his way.

"Marina wouldn't accept there was anything wrong," Dan said, frustration knitting his brow. It was unusual for him to encounter a problem he couldn't solve. Although his job title was import and export manager, he was Marty's troubleshooter, and he was good at it.

"We shouldn't be surprised," Marty said. "She's never been interested in the dirty business of manufacturing, only in spending the profits."

"I emailed Marina to say we had to destroy the entire container-load, and wouldn't pay for it," Dan said. "I got a reply straight back. The gist of it was, either we pay up or she won't supply to us again."

Marty whistled. She had to be bluffing. "I'll call her," he said. "Meanwhile, we're out of pocket, and short of stock. We paid tax on that vodka when it came out of bond."

"We can get the excise duty back," Dan assured him. "Stock levels are more of a problem, but I can manage customers' expectations as long as I know when the next shipment's coming."

"Leave it with me," Marty said. He checked his watch as Dan left. It was nearly lunchtime in Bazakistan. Marina might well have stopped work for the day, to visit an exclusive boutique or have a beauty treatment before clubbing in the centre of Kireniat with her latest lover. He didn't care. Her staff knew he was their biggest customer, and they'd track her down for him. She might try to fob Dan off, but it wouldn't work on Marty. He rang the Snow Mountain switchboard.

As expected, he was connected to Marina within minutes.

"Marty, what's this nonsense I hear from your boy?" The distillery owner was clearly uninterested in small talk.

"I could ask you the same," Marty said. "Letting methanol into your product is a serious breach of quality control. It could be fatal to the Snow Mountain brand, to your business, and most of all, to consumers."

Marina sneered. "Obviously," she said. "But this is merely your ploy to avoid paying me, isn't it? You're trying to get the shipment for free."

"If only that were true," Marty said. "Will you believe me when I send the paperwork proving the shipment's been destroyed? I need all that anyway for the UK customs and excise."

Marina laughed. "Documents can be faked."

Marty was losing patience. "Well then, send one of your engineers over here, and they can see for themselves. They can test as many bottles as they want. And before you make ridiculous allegations about tampering, I can get another case straight out of bond for them to sample."

"Grigor will be on the first flight from Kireniat to Heathrow tomorrow morning," Marina said. "If I find out you're cheating me, I'm getting another distributor."

"I own the brand," Marty said. "There is no one else who can distribute Snow Mountain. But let's be clear, if you send any more rubbish my way, I'll get another supplier. Clean up your act, or your business will go down the toilet."

"Enough," Marina snapped. "We'll see what Grigor has to say. He's my chief engineer, and you won't fool him."

Marty left it at that. There was more he could have said. Marina had, after all, mounted a legal challenge to his ownership of the worldwide brand rights for Snow Mountain. He was defending his intellectual property, but the product contamination could be an attempt to discourage him. If so, it was a risky strategy on her part. There was a strong chance she'd destroy the brand's reputation in the process, and what good would it do her then?

Since the fall of the Soviet Union, Bazakistan had built an economy from mineral rights and agriculture, but products like Snow Mountain vodka were still perceived as valuable exports by the nation's ageing President. Would Marina, a self-styled patriot, escape official censure if those exports vanished overnight, whether by scheming or carelessness? Marty thought not.

The most plausible explanation was that Marina's production team had cut corners. They'd have let the methanol through in a bid to squeeze more output from the plant. It was an amateurish mistake. Kat, her daughter, would never have done that. Even when Kat had made vodka in a small cellar with a Heath Robinson-type tangle of pipes, the spirit had been exceptionally pure.

Marty's lips tightened. Tim, his eldest son, had persuaded him to invest in Kat's new vodka brand. She was about to begin production in premises on the other side of the city centre. With a little more time, he could have asked Kat to make Snow Mountain for him. Whatever Marina thought, he owned the brand. Still, vodka produced in Birmingham would be perceived differently by consumers than a spirit crafted in the tree-lined hills of Bazakistan.

Anyway, who knew whether Kat would agree? And how trustworthy was she? Like her father, Sasha Belov, she could make the best vodka in the world. But what devious genes had Kat inherited from Marina? He should have kept well away from Marina's daughter and made sure Tim did the same.

Somehow, he had to resolve this supply problem, and soon. Snow Mountain was the bedrock of his drinks business, accounting for ten per cent of East West Bridges' sales, but half of its profit. It didn't just underpin his own lifestyle, but that of his employees, including three of his four children.

That wasn't all. Marty relied on East West Bridges to fund a cancer research joint venture. A high six figure payment was required to start more clinical trials soon. Where would he find it if income from Snow Mountain took a dive?

"I'm taking an early lunch, Tanya. Hair of the dog," he told his PA. His temples throbbed. Caffeine and sugar had merely nibbled at the edges of the headache. A pint of bitter and a pork pie at the Craven Arms would restore him.

Sweating, despite leaving his suit jacket behind, he strode into the sunshine. Viewed from outside, the single storey office was as unlovely as the old warehouse behind it. He'd bought the premises cheaply, though; while Florence Street was a short walk from the centre of Birmingham, it was in a crumbling industrial enclave.

10

As usual, little disturbed the hot summer air. Marty barely noticed the rhythmic thud of a small workshop's machines down the road, and the clatter of a courier firm's metal shutter opposite.

Lost in thought, he crossed the street. Suddenly, he turned at the loud rattle of a diesel engine. One of the courier's vans was heading straight towards him. Instinct raised his hands to shield his head, while desperation sent him leaping to one side. Still, the white van bore down.

The vehicle screeched to a halt, its tyres smoking. An acrid smell of burnt rubber filled the air. It had missed him by inches.

"Use your eyes," he yelled, as the driver waved a tanned hand and sped off around the corner.

Hajji, the young gopher at Hero Couriers, emerged from behind the shutter. "Sorry, Mr Bridges," he said. "He's new. I'll get the boss to have a word with him."

"Get him to watch where he's going," Marty said. His racing heart had quieted now. "Look, I know time is money for your guys, okay? Just apply some common sense. And tell your boss he owes me a discount."

The pub's siren call lured him even more strongly. When he discovered there had been no delivery of pork pies that day, he was reminded of the adage that troubles come in threes. Unlike the vodka contamination or the over-enthusiastic courier, this setback was easy to address. Marty ordered an extra pint of beer. Briefly, all was well with the world.

Chapter 2.　　　　　Kat

A horn sounded as Kat White entered the three-storey redbrick building. It was one of the properties Marty appeared to keep, like cards in his pocket, dotted around the fringes of the city centre. The alarm system was a recent addition, installed to protect her precious Starshine vodka. Its noise ceased when she tapped a combination into a pad.

The air was heavy with a sweet, cloying smell, halfway between a brewery and a chip shop. This was the aroma of fermented potatoes. When Kat had first used them for vodka, the odour had made her gag. Those days were well past, along with the demijohns employed in her initial experiments. Marty's money had bought professional distilling equipment, including huge stainless steel tanks. One of these contained the rough brew. Having lain in the tank for six days, it was ready for its first distillation this morning.

Kat had been a daddy's girl, following her father around his distillery as a small child. It meant she had complete faith that the dirt-coloured alcoholic broth could be turned into a pure, clean spirit.

Humming, she flicked a switch to send the soupy liquid down a pipe into the stripper. This was a column made of steel, with a boiler beneath it, stretching up for two storeys. Marty and his sons had reconfigured the building, knocking the ceilings through at one end and installing ladders. The full height of the property was required for the stripper and its big brother, the rectification column, which Kat would use later.

The boiler thrummed into life. As the lumpy soup bubbled, its alcohol evaporated, travelling to the top of the stripper for collection in a condenser. This cooled the gas into a liquid again. The distillate was too strong to drink, and anyway, it was rougher than the worst moonshine. Kat didn't plan to dip a finger in it. Instead, she sent the raw spirit travelling through another pipe to Sasha.

Her face flushed with pride as she turned her attention to the polished copper still. Had she followed tradition in the industry, it would have had a female name. Kat, however, had christened hers after her late father. Alexander Belov had always been Sasha to his family and friends.

This Sasha was thirsty, demanding plenty of water for the second distillation. Kat had been delighted to find that Birmingham's water came from the Welsh mountains. Its softness and purity were superior even to the stream from which Alexander Belov had drawn his supplies.

Sasha's alchemy transformed moonshine and water into something magical. Only the final rectification was required now: the third distillation in a column seventy feet high. For the next couple of hours, Kat concentrated on this. She drew away the first vapours to emerge. These were the heads, containing deadly methanol.

Next, she allowed the hearts, the vodka she wanted to keep, to flow into the maturation tank. Every twenty minutes or so, she tasted a sample to be sure it was still clean and creamy.

Her finely-tuned palate told her when the hearts were coming to an end. Immediately, Kat switched outflow pipes, sending the rest of the production run down the drain. This was the tails: not poisonous, but unpleasant to drink.

In two weeks, she'd be emptying the maturation tank into Starshine vodka bottles for the very first time. Excitement sustained her as she worked without a break until mid-afternoon. Only then did she realise how uncomfortably warm the room had become. Kat shrugged off her lab coat. Stopping for a quick shot of instant coffee, she spent the rest of the day cleaning the equipment.

She was still high on adrenaline as she walked home. For most of her twenty-six years, she'd dreamed of running a high-end vodka business. Thanks to Tim, it was starting to happen.

Although Marty had driven a hard bargain when he invested in the Starshine joint venture, he wouldn't have considered it all without his son to win him over. Kat thanked fate for sending Tim on a Snow Mountain sales call to the casino where she'd been working. The romance it had sparked had turned into something even more life-changing.

She marched quickly, determined to arrive home and make a start decorating before Tim visited. The crumbling Victorian redbrick semi near the Edgbaston Reservoir had seen better days. While she couldn't change its shabby exterior, she'd decided to give her rented bedsit a facelift.

His sporty gold Subaru drew alongside just as she rounded a corner and the grungy house, its front garden thick with weeds, came into view.

He wound down the window and grinned, a summer breeze teasing his waxed fair hair. "Thought I'd stop by early and give you a hand. Does that meet with your approval, Katya Belova?"

"It does, Timothy Bridges." She looked away, wincing, her hand trembling as she unlocked the peeling grey front door. Nobody used her birth name anymore. She was a British citizen now, her surname changed by deed poll. If she counted her time at the posh boarding school she'd been forced to leave at sixteen, she'd lived in England for more than half her life.

She might preserve memories of her dead father, but there were other fragments of the past she preferred to forget.

Tim put a hand on her shoulder. "Have I spoken out of turn?" he asked softly.

"No," she lied, before changing the subject. "Guess what? I distilled my first commercial batch of Starshine today."

Tim's handsome face lit up at the news. "Then let's go to the pub to celebrate. We'll get the decorating done in an hour."

Kat laughed. "Are you sure? You must be a quick worker."

"I've brought paint pads. They're much faster to use than brushes. I know what I'm doing. Dad had us all decorating as soon as we could walk."

Kat wasn't surprised that Marty had used his children as free labour. Even now, he didn't pay Tim the market rate for his job as a sales director.

Tim took a holdall from his car and followed her into the lobby and up the stairs to the first floor. The communal area was tatty but inoffensive. Kat had blu-tacked cheap botanical prints to the scuffed white walls. Occasionally, she sprayed air freshener to banish a lingering whiff of mould.

Her own flat, at the back of the first floor, smelled of new paint. As soon as they entered it, she opened the single large sash window, infusing the air with perfume from roses in the garden below.

"You've done the woodwork already. Nice job."

"It took me all weekend," Kat said.

"This won't." Tim unpacked his holdall and stretched to his full height, just under six foot. "Here are the pads. I'll change into my sexy boiler suit, then I'll show you how it's done."

Within ninety minutes, the damp-stained primrose yellow walls were covered in pale pink. Tim laid his paint pad on a wad of newspaper.

"It's looking good," he said, "although this Angel's Kiss isn't my scene." His apartment, in a classier district, was tricked out in a modern monochrome style.

"We've got Parma Violet, Phantom Dream and Hazy Sky left," Kat said, reading the labels of the smaller pots stacked neatly by the door. "We could do up the furniture next. What do you say?"

The pieces in the room were old, and of chipped brown wood. She couldn't wait to transform them, and replace the faded carpet with painted boards.

Tim's blue eyes twinkled. "I'd say it's time we went to the pub."

"All right," Kat said. "I'll do the rest tomorrow. And pop over to the Rag Market at the weekend for a couple of cotton rugs."

"Nice," Tim said, his tone suggesting a polite lack of interest.

"We could take a picnic to the reservoir now, though. It'll be more fun than the pubs around here." Kat favoured the more upmarket watering holes of the Jewellery Quarter. "I've got everything we need – a baguette, cheese, white wine."

"Beer?" he asked.

"A few bottles of Two Towers Hockley Gold. Am I the perfect woman, or what?" She knew it was the drink Tim favoured. Marty Bridges made his money from vodka, but he'd always loved real ale, and had brought up his sons to do the same.

Kat packed a bag of food and drink in her tiny kitchen, then popped into the even smaller bathroom off it to make sure she looked presentable. She combed and fluffed her long blonde hair, accentuating her green eyes with jet-black mascara and liner and slicking red gloss on her lips. Her jeans and white T-shirt were smart enough for a picnic, having escaped the paint.

By the time she returned, Tim was back in his business suit. He closed the window. "You want to watch your security, Kat. You can't be too careful. After all, you've been threatened by a jailbird before."

"I wanted to air the place while we were out." As she said it, a quiver of alarm needled her spine. The flat felt like a safe haven, but could she ever be sure Shaun Halloran wouldn't find her? He'd managed it twice already.

Tim was speaking again, oblivious to her fears. "Air will still get in, because your sash is so draughty. You'll freeze to death in the winter. Large rooms like this are fine in my father's house with his central heating, but you'll have nothing to keep you warm."

"Except you," Kat said, squeezing his hand. She forgot all her concerns, desire seizing her as she touched him and gazed into his eyes.

15

The whole package was appealing: his athletic body, wavy hair and tanned skin.

"Behave," Tim said. "Time for that later, when the paint's dry. I'm not staying here to watch it with beer on offer. I want to get down the rezzer before nightfall." He laughed as she looked askance. "We'll make a Brummie of you yet."

Apart from a few dialect words, he didn't really sound like a Brummie himself. Tim had won a scholarship to an exclusive school, and the Birmingham accent sported by the rest of the Bridges family had been refined out of him. He'd inherited Marty's natural ambition, though. Kat saw him as a kindred spirit: she, too, was driven to succeed. It was exciting to be working with Tim on their new project. If anyone could sell Starshine Vodka, it was him. He'd cut his teeth in business selling Snow Mountain for his father, a task that still took up most of his time.

Fingers intertwined, they walked towards the reservoir, past once-grand villas carved into multiple dwellings, newer box-like houses and the car park that fringed one edge of the square stretch of water. Beyond this, they found a bench from which to view a small boat sailing lazily across the shimmering ripples.

A light breeze cut through the July heat, whipping Kat's hair in front of her eyes. Her lover flicked it back and kissed her.

She handed Tim a bottle of beer and divided up the food, giving most of it to him. She didn't need the calories. There were enough in the glass of dry white wine she poured herself, opening a bottle still misted from resting in the fridge.

"This area's too rundown for you," Tim said. "I meant what I said about the winter, too. You should move out before the weather gets cold."

"It never climbs above zero in Bazakistan for three whole months of the year," Kat said. "Anyway, after everything I've done to the flat, my landlord won't release my deposit."

Tim snorted. "You're joking, aren't you? It was a dump before and now it's almost habitable."

She shivered, chilled by her misgivings rather than the breeze. Was Tim criticising the neighbourhood because he wanted her to move in with him? She wouldn't do it, despite the pang of loneliness that always seared through her when he had to leave.

A year ago, she'd been left with little more than the clothes on her back when she split from Ross, her fiancé. Now, her personal and

16

business relationships with Tim were already messily entangled. If they became any closer, she'd risk being hurt worse than ever before.

Chapter 3.   Marty

"Mr Vlasenko's here," Tanya said, entering Marty's office with a tray containing cafetière, cups, cream and sugar. She set them out on the meeting table.

Marty nodded to his PA, clocking a new hairstyle, then looked at his watch. "He's early. Good. Bring him in."

He dimly recalled meeting Grigor before at the distillery. The man had worked at the Snow Mountain distillery since leaving the local university. One of the ethnic Russians who had settled in Bazakistan, he must be pushing forty. He'd been promoted to chief engineer under Harry Aliyev. In effect, he was now the factory manager, although his pay wouldn't reflect it. Marina hadn't hired anyone to replace her late husband at the distillery's helm, and she certainly hadn't taken over his duties herself.

The strong aroma of coffee, a dark Italian blend that Tanya tracked down specially for Marty, was too good to resist. Marty helped himself to a cup just as Grigor was being ushered into the room.

The chief engineer, smartly dressed in a suit like Marty, his dark hair and beard neatly trimmed, swaggered over with his hand outstretched. "How are you?" he said in Russian. "Your secretary – is her hair the fashion here?"

Marty laughed. "It's just as well she doesn't speak Russian," he said, matching Grigor's language. "No, a bright pink pixie cut is a trend all her own." It was the single distinctive feature of Tanya's otherwise unremarkable middle-aged appearance.

"Nice office, by the way."

"Thanks." New visitors rarely expected to see a room like this, panelled and furnished in bird's eye maple, the cream carpet and picture windows pristine. The view of the adjacent car park was unspectacular, but at least it allowed Marty to admire his gleaming Jaguar.

Marty filled the second cup with coffee, and placed it in front of an S-shaped meeting seat. He returned to his higher and more luxurious leather swivel chair, stretching his feet out onto the desk. He steepled his hands beneath his chin. Continuing in fluent Russian, he said, "Enough of the small talk. What has Marina told you?"

Grigor, now seated and looking up at him, grimaced. "You think my product's contaminated. It's highly unlikely, to be honest."

"Look at the test results." Marty swivelled his laptop around, so Grigor could see the email in which Dan had set them out. "There's methanol in your latest batch. Here's the result of our test on the consignment before, so you can compare them. That one's clean."

"Your son did these himself?"

"Yes, he spot-checks using refractive index measurement to start with, then moves on to more sophisticated and costly methods if he has to. We've never found anything before, but we're not complacent, and just as well."

"A refractometer's not good enough," Grigor protested. "Our quality assurance is based on chromatography."

"We went one better, actually. This time, to be certain, Dan took a bottle to a third party lab with a mass spectrometer. It confirmed our suspicions. Anyway, whatever system you're using, it didn't work, did it?"

Grigor shook his head. "Marina wants more proof than this." He gestured to Marty's laptop.

"She can have whatever she needs. I'll call Dan here and, together, you can test another bottle."

"You're coming too," Grigor said. "I want you to see that my vodka is as pure as an angel's heart."

"Very well." Marty finished his coffee. "Ready?"

They walked past the cubicles and shared office spaces where Marty's staff worked in surroundings less grand than his. Beyond these was the cavernous warehouse, with its sawtooth corrugated roof.

"Here's Dan," Marty said, spotting his second son giving instructions to a forklift truck driver. "We'll have to swap to English now, as it's the only language he knows."

"I speak pure Brummie, actually," Dan said, a remark that went over Grigor's head.

"Grigor, Dan," Marty said. "Grigor wants to test a bottle of the latest Snow Mountain. Can you help him find one?"

"These crates here," Dan said. He pointed to some paperwork clipped to one of the boxes. "That's what we had this week."

Grigor inspected the documents and took a bottle. "This one," he said, ignoring Marty's instruction to speak English.

"Right, we'll put it through the refractometer," Dan said.

Grigor nodded. He seemed to understand.

19

Dan led them to the lab, a pocket-sized, windowless room next to a toilet. He showed Grigor the refractometer. To Marty's eyes, it looked like a piece of office equipment: a white plastic box with a screen on the front and a few switches.

Grigor opened the bottle, squinting at the label. He winced.

"What's wrong?" Marty asked.

"Nothing," Grigor mumbled. "This was a special batch, that's all. I didn't realise there was any of it in your consignment. Anyway, it doesn't matter, because there's nothing wrong with it."

Dan measured a small sample, and poured it through a funnel into the machine. "The moment of truth," he said.

Grigor paled as the screen displayed its result.

"Do you need to sit down?" Marty asked, waving at a chair.

"No," Grigor stammered. "Just a stomach upset. I need to visit the restroom."

"Next door," Marty said.

The chief engineer rushed out. Marty held a finger across his lips. The partition wall didn't quite meet the lab's ceiling. If someone listened carefully, they could hear a conversation in the adjacent room: a telephone call, for instance.

"…cancel the party…throw it away…" he heard Grigor say before the toilet was flushed.

"Do you want to do further tests?" Marty asked, when Grigor reappeared.

"No, I've seen enough," Grigor said.

"Dan, that's all for now," Marty said. "Grigor and I will have a private chat in my office." As they walked back, he asked the engineer, "Do you want more coffee? Or something stronger?"

"Neat vodka, but not from that bottle," Grigor said. He seemed almost broken. The swagger was gone.

Marty stopped at Tanya's workstation to request more coffee anyway.

"Well," he said, when he was back at his desk, with hot drinks in front of them, "are you going to tell her?"

"It's been done. I'm sure I'll lose my job over this."

Marty wondered if that was the only reason Grigor's skin was ashen below that dark beard. "What's the significance of this batch?" he asked. "You said it wasn't for export."

Grigor shifted in his seat. "There's a party at the distillery tonight, to mark the twenty-fifth anniversary of Snow Mountain. Marina Aliyeva reserved vodka for it, to serve at the function and hand out as gifts. We took special care in making it."

Somebody had, Marty thought. "Who's going?" he asked.

"VIPs," Grigor said. "Dina. She's top of the hit parade," he added, in response to a blank look from Marty. "The Mayor of Kireniat, as well. Rumour has it that the President himself will be there."

"I see. Could Marina Aliyeva herself be responsible for the impurities?" Marty asked.

Grigor gawped. "I shouldn't think so," he said. "She's never had anything to do with our manufacturing process: not while Belov or Aliyev were around, and not now either. Why should she?"

"Why indeed?" Marty said. "At the very least, I'd expect her to take an interest in quality control."

"She doesn't have that background," Grigor said.

It was a reasonable statement. Marina Aliyeva's skills were mostly horizontal, or, if Marty were being charitable, those of a secret policeman at best.

"What does she spend her time doing?" Marty asked.

Grigor shrugged. "Seeing her Government friends," he said.

"Including the President's son?" Marty saw from the flicker in Grigor's eyes that he'd hit the bullseye. "I suppose the old man's got to name a successor soon," he added. "May as well keep it in the family." He could hardly criticise the Bazaki ruler's nepotism: he planned to pass his own business to his children one day.

"I know nothing of such things," Grigor said. "What does concern me is our production problem. This shouldn't happen. We have safeguards."

Marty stared at him.

Grigor squirmed. "I'll go back today and start investigating our processes. But I've got other shipments making their way on trains through Europe at the moment." His eyes were troubled. "We won't know if they're contaminated until they arrive."

"I'm not accepting them," Marty said.

He couldn't take the risk. It didn't matter whether it was sabotage or carelessness that had caused the contamination. He wouldn't buy vodka from Marina Aliyeva again.

21

Whatever the damage to his finances, he couldn't afford to. If Dan hadn't spotted it, that special vodka would have killed somebody.

Chapter 4.   Kat

"Yes, I'll be there at four." Kat didn't waste words on Marty. She expected him to give more than an hour's notice if he wanted a meeting. It was a question of respect. He'd put capital into their Starshine vodka joint venture, but she owned half of the company. She was doing all the work too, and for little reward.

Still, it was a pleasant walk to his office through Birmingham city centre, its streets glistening in sunshine after a sharp rain shower. Kat enjoyed window-shopping in the kind of boutiques where she would have spent hundreds of pounds on Ross's credit card without thinking twice. Those designer dresses were way above her budget now. Anyway, she dressed casually for her work as a distiller.

Kat scanned the East West Bridges car park for Tim's Subaru before remembering he'd driven to Manchester that morning. He was visiting a string of customers in the north-west. Marty's silver Jag dominated the tarmac, a diamond in the rough among the Corsas and Skodas surrounding it.

Marty, as usual, was playing mind games. He stayed in his executive chair when Tanya shepherded Kat into his office. "Pull up a pew," he said.

Kat sat opposite him, noting that she was positioned nearer to the ground. He must have adjusted his seat to tower over her.

"Coffee?" Tanya asked.

"Always. Yes, please; black," Kat said before Marty could utter a word. She'd beat him at his own game.

"Bring biccies too, please, Tanya," Marty requested.

Kat waited until Tanya had left. "What's going on, Marty?"

"I thought you deserved a pay rise."

She tried not to show her astonishment. "At least double," Kat said.

"Let's say twenty per cent to start with." Marty leaned forward. "Now you've proved you can get Starshine production up and running without a glitch, I'd like to invest in more capacity. Your factory unit is virtually empty. We can fit four times as much kit in there."

So that was why he'd suggested paying more; he wanted to quadruple her workload. "I'll need to recruit, then," Kat said. "Two qualified distillers, minimum."

Tanya arrived with the coffee tray, placing it on Marty's desk before leaving the room.

"Mmm, Illy from Italy," Marty said. "Shall I be mother?" He hit the cafetière plunger and poured the dark liquid into two white china cups, handing Kat a plate of shortbread fingers.

She waved them away.

"Suit yourself," Marty said cheerfully, helping himself to a couple. He added cream and sugar to his coffee.

Kat sipped her drink. "What's your budget for new equipment? And for extra sales support?"

"Sales is Tim's area, but there's no need to change what we're doing at the moment. I take it you're satisfied with Tim's services?" Marty winked.

Kat forced herself not to blush. "Yes, but he'll have to spend more time on Starshine if I ramp up production."

"Not necessarily," Marty said. "I want you to make Snow Mountain vodka, not Starshine."

Kat jumped to her feet. "In Birmingham? You've mentioned that idea before, and I thought it was a joke. Snow Mountain is a Bazaki brand, crafted in the countryside from local grain and mountain stream water."

"And methanol," Marty said.

"What?" This made no sense.

"Your mother sent me a shipment laced with methanol," Marty said.

Kat gasped. She already regarded her mother as lost to her. Who could forgive the woman who had betrayed her husband and abandoned her children? This was worse, though. "She's playing with people's lives."

"Lucky we caught it," Marty said. "But I can't buy from her again. This wouldn't have happened if Sasha was around. He was my best friend, as well as a superb distiller. I miss him, as I'm sure you do."

"Don't guilt-trip me," Kat said, with vehemence.

"No guilt-tripping intended," Marty said. "You share Sasha's talents, and together, we can fix the problem. Yes, I know Starshine and Snow Mountain have different recipes, but you can make them side by side. Birmingham tap water is as pure as any river in Bazakistan."

"It'll never take off," Kat said. "Where's the brand integrity? Anyway, what's Snow Mountain to me? I don't have a stake in it. Starshine has my heart and soul. If I stop concentrating on that, it will suffer."

Marty stood up too. The difference in height was less marked than when they'd been seated; he was only an inch or so taller than her.

"Brand integrity?" he said, his face reddening as he thrust it towards hers. "Let the marketing guys worry about that. Your friend, Amy, and Tim, for example. You need to realise that Snow Mountain should be everything to you. It's what pays for all this." He stretched out his arms. "This office, this warehouse, and your craft distillery with its shiny new pipes."

"Starshine is going places," Kat said. "I can't afford to lose focus."

"So that's your final answer?" Marty glared. "Think on it, when the money runs out. If I go bankrupt, your precious Starshine goes down with me."

Chapter 5.   Marty

Darria Enterprises was a few minutes' walk from the Rose Villa Tavern, a handsome redbrick gothic pub in Birmingham's Jewellery Quarter. While the cancer drug business was a joint venture, Marty mostly left his partner to his own devices. Erik White wasn't just a talented scientist, but a farmer who was growing the darria herb from which the experimental drug was synthesised. Marty's only role was to apply financial rigour.

By the time Erik arrived at 6pm, Marty had already bought beer for them both and found a quiet corner.

"Sorry I'm late," Erik said. "I was so absorbed in the British Medical Journal, I lost track of time. How are you doing?"

"I've got less hair than a week ago." Marty took a swig of his pint. There was no easy way of saying it. "Erik, this business isn't paying its way. We'd planned to sell darria tea to cover the cost of further clinical trials, but it's not happening. Although sales were promising to start with, they've taken a dip."

"Any idea why?" Erik asked. Golden light streamed through the pub's ornate stained glass windows, lending a halo to his black spiky hair. Tall, thin and pale, he looked like his father's ghost.

"Consumers are chasing the next fad," Marty said. "My wife swears by darria to keep her looking young, but Angela alone can't keep the business afloat." She did her best, though, drinking the foul-tasting brew morning and night.

"Never mind," Erik said. "The anti-ageing tea is a side hustle. Once we get a licence for the cancer drug, we won't look back."

Marty sighed. "I can't afford the next round of trials, Erik. Not unless I sell all my property investments and mortgage my house, and even then, maybe not. The cost you quoted in your last email was twice what I'd budgeted. But that's not all. I face a crisis with my Snow Mountain supply."

"What do you mean?"

"Your mother sent me a consignment contaminated with methanol. I can't trust her to do it again."

Erik's expression was bleak. "Nobody can trust her," he said. "So, without Snow Mountain sales, your cashflow's weak."

"Worse than weak. It's negative."

"I guess I'd better put my research on hold until you can overcome the vodka problems. And sell more tea."

Marty nodded, relieved that Erik was so different from his younger sister. Where Kat was self-centred, quiet Erik would listen and compromise.

Erik grimaced. "I can delay for a few months to defer the cost. I wouldn't wish to wait much longer. Have you spoken to my sister?"

"I asked her to make Snow Mountain for me. I offered her a pay rise, even though I'll be borrowing to pay the wages this month. She refused to help."

Erik clearly sensed Marty's frustration. "Let me talk to Kat. And I'll see if my girlfriend can persuade her. Amy and Kat are having a girls' weekend in London soon."

"I'm obviously paying them too much," Marty said.

"They won't be splashing the cash," Erik said. "Amy's father invited them to London to help plan his second wedding. Amy's a bridesmaid."

"They're having a big do, aren't they?" Marty said. "A top London hotel with views of the Thames. Champagne before, during and after. It'll cost a pretty penny."

"You seem to know a lot about the arrangements. Has Amy shared them with everyone at your office?"

"I'm getting an invitation myself. Charles and Dee told me to save the date," Marty said. "You remember, when Amy came to work for me, Charles insisted on visiting? He wanted to check us out. We met for a drink a couple of times after that."

"I can see why you'd get on. Charles likes his craft beer."

"Angela's really excited about attending a celebrity wedding. It's giving her kudos with the ladies who lunch."

Erik grinned. "Dee's yoga DVDs must be popular with that crowd. How about you?"

"Yoga? No thanks. The wedding will give me a chance to tell Dee and her famous friends about darria tea. If they promote it to their hordes of social media followers, we can turn the business around." Marty chuckled. "I'll get Amy on the case."

"She's supposed to be marketing vodka."

"When there is any." Marty swallowed the rest of his pint, and went to the bar for another. His vodka supply was still uncertain, along with his finances. At least Erik's cancer research wasn't about to soak up millions he didn't have.

Chapter 6.   Ben

Ben Halloran sipped his coffee and selected a Glock 17 pistol. Did it have a safety catch? No; it was an excellent choice. He pulled the trigger.

Blood and brains spattered everywhere, right to the edge of the screen. The stats at the bottom said it was his 141st zombie kill: just as well, because he'd lost count.

Although he earned his living playing fantasy games, he could hold his own in shoot'em ups. He enjoyed chilling in this Hackney café, checking out new games and catching up with the guys.

In real life, he wasn't a lawman with an unlimited selection of weapons at his disposal, but a skinny twentysomething with floppy brown hair. His background was very different from the avatar disposing of zombies.

Ben sighed. He had to meet Vince, who was a link with his childhood, and not in a good way. Logging out, he waved to his fellow enthusiasts. "See you tomorrow."

"Laters."

In August, the café was busier on a Friday than usual. The handful of veterans, Ben's age and above, had been joined by adolescents who were usually at school. One or two were even girls. A few lads glanced out of the window after him, obviously admiring the new black Golf GTi he'd parked right outside. Ben wondered if gaming was their safety valve, as it had been for him as a teenager.

As a gamer, you were the hero of your own legend. His earliest memories were of sitting on his father's knee, listening to stories of bravery and cunning. Like the fairytales Ben's mother read to him, Shaun Halloran's yarns were fantastical: anecdotes of rivals buried alive in the foundations of shopping centres, and the police being outwitted.

Ben had treated the information as colourful fiction. He was perhaps ten years old when he realised from the reactions of his schoolmates that Shaun's stories were true. At about the same time, he did his SATS at primary school. He'd found the tests easier than everyone else. His mother had been delighted. Unexpectedly, his father wasn't. Shaun couldn't understand why a child should have his nose in books.

Ben had naively hoped Shaun would be pleased when books were replaced by PCs and games consoles. It hadn't taken long to learn otherwise. Again, his father couldn't see how or why Ben's interests should lead to a career. Shaun enjoyed the excitement of running an empire of drug runners, drinks dens and shady ladies. Why wouldn't Ben want a part of that? Ben's preference for a virtual world was a source of disappointment.

He couldn't remember when he'd stopped idolising his dad, shutting himself in his room to avoid arguments and violence. It gave him no pleasure to think how far his father had fallen as his own star had risen: the despised video games having taken Ben all over the world, while Shaun's empire had shrunk to a Belmarsh prison cell.

Now, driving to Hoxton to meet his father's wingman, he saw a blue light in his mirror. Here we go, he thought. He pulled over on a double yellow line.

The patrol car stopped behind him. A policeman emerged, strutting towards the Golf, self-important in a stab vest and silly hat. Ben noticed the officer remaining in the vehicle was female. She was preoccupied with a phone or tablet.

Ben opened his window, recognising the young cop as he did so. Kyle Lassiter had been a school prefect, and officious with it.

"Good morning, Sir," Lassiter said, a smirk appearing between his protruding chin and the monobrow that sat like a black caterpillar on his forehead. "You appear to be parked on a double yellow line."

"I thought you wanted me to stop," Ben said.

"Where safe and legal to do so," Lassiter told him. His lip twisted into a sneer.

Ben felt nothing but contempt. There was no point being angry. He'd had many encounters of this sort. His surname attracted them. "Sorry, Kyle," he said. "I can move along if you like."

"Oh, it's Ben Halloran, isn't it?" As if Lassiter didn't know. "How come a scruffy university drop-out like you can afford to drive a GTi? Doing a bit of dealing, are you?"

Ben didn't give Lassiter the satisfaction of a reaction. "I won it in a competition," he said, coolly.

"Is that so?" Lassiter said. He nodded to his colleague in the car behind. It, too, was squatting on double yellows. "We'll just run a check on this vehicle. I'll have your driving licence and your keys, please."

Ben handed over the fob. He could still have driven away with a press of the push-start button. Didn't Lassiter appreciate that?

The licence was in his wallet. Ben reached into the inside breast pocket of his black leather jacket, retrieving a passport as well.

"Let me see that too," Lassiter snapped.

Ben was tempted to say that Lassiter knew who he was, but kept his mouth shut. When your opponent held all the aces, silence was the best policy. He gave both documents to the policeman.

Lassiter pretended to scrutinise them in minute detail. "Hmm. Not obvious forgeries," he said. He flicked through the passport, looking Ben up and down. The photograph, Ben's blue eyes staring straight at the camera under a long brown fringe, was an exceptionally clear likeness. Lassiter wouldn't find anything amiss.

"I see you've been travelling," Lassiter observed. "Korea, Japan and Dubai. What were you doing there?"

It was none of Lassiter's business, but Ben didn't mind answering. "Video game tournaments," he said. "I make a living from eSports." Perhaps Lassiter really had no idea. The policeman had always been a rugby player rather than a computer nerd. Since they left school, their paths hadn't crossed.

Lassiter's companion emerged from their vehicle. She was probably also in her early twenties, and a lot prettier than Lassiter, her hazel eyes dominating a pale, heart-shaped face. Wisps of dark hair escaped from a bun under her bowler hat. Lassiter would be showing off to her.

The policeman frowned. "I thought I told you to stay in there, Nat."

"I wanted to stretch my legs," Nat said.

Ben couldn't help ogling them. Lassiter responded with a malicious stare.

"The Golf's taxed and insured. Owned by Benjamin Michael Halloran," Nat said. "I imagine that squares with the driving licence."

"Yes, it does," Lassiter conceded, with bad grace.

"Thought so." She smiled, revealing perfect white teeth. "I googled the name as well. He won the car in a computer game tournament."

At least she was behaving like an adult. She, for one, would understand the stamps on his passport, and might even know they didn't match traditional drug supply lines. There was every chance she knew Lassiter was an idiot.

Lassiter scowled, returning the documents and fob. "Very well. Everything seems to be in order. Drive on."

"Thanks, Kyle." Ben was careful to sound more polite than he felt. Kyle Lassiter had the might of the Met on his side. Ben had no one.

He left the window open as he started the car, and had the uncertain pleasure of overhearing Nat say to Lassiter, "I don't know why we had to stop him, Kyle. He seemed okay. A zaddy, even."

Lassiter grunted. "When's your eye test? You can't trust a Halloran."

The GTi pulled away swiftly. Ben parked in Hoxton Square a few minutes later; too soon for his liking. Although the encounter with Lassiter had been annoying, the forthcoming meeting with Vince invoked a deep sense of unease. Ben could handle Vince's hipster pretensions and hot temper, but not the knowledge that everything they planned was a step further back to his father's world.

Vince wasn't in the bar yet. Ben bought a beer and found a table. Nearby, two pretty girls, a blonde and a redhead, were sipping cocktails. Ben's mood lifted. Perhaps he could enjoy himself while he waited.

Chapter 7.   Kat

"I miss London bars," Amy said. She beamed, scanning the cocktail joint in Hoxton, twisting a tendril of long red hair around her finger, and sipping a drink, all at the same time.

Kat laughed. "Changed your tune, haven't you?" she said. "Ever since you moved there, you've been singing Birmingham's praises."

Amy blushed. "Brum has its advantages. Erik, for example." He was Kat's brother, and Amy's partner.

"We could have brought him with us for the weekend. Or maybe not. Two's company, three's a crowd."

"This pub is awesome. It's really cheap." Amy had homed in on a bar on Hoxton Square. The cocktail prices were scarcely higher than their local in Birmingham.

"It's happy hour," Kat said. "I prefer Charlotte Street - less gritty, and more central." It was the lane of bars and boutiques in Fitzrovia, the London enclave just north of Soho, where she'd lived with Ross. Going out there was expensive, but it hadn't mattered when he was paying.

"Still, it's nice of Dad to lend us his place," Amy said. "Just as well it was free." Having moved into his fiancée's gracious house in suburbia, her father rented out his hip flat in Shoreditch. It was currently between tenants.

"It's not a swanky hotel, but it's better than his spare room in Primrose Hill," Kat said. "Imagine that. All yummy mummies and baby sick there."

"And little George waking up in the night," Amy said. "He's cute until he cries. Then I give him back."

"No thanks," Kat said, with a shudder.

"Dee's turned into Bridezilla, too," Amy said. "Don't let me get lashed, Kat, because I'm seeing her to talk dresses tomorrow." She beamed. "I always dreamed of being a bridesmaid. I never thought it would be at my father's wedding."

"How does your mum feel about it?"

"She's not going. She doesn't regret her divorce, but she says it's weird to celebrate when he marries someone else."

"Charles lucked out when he met Dee," Kat said. "She must be loaded."

"Yes, and it's her first marriage, so it's money no object. The hen weekend is a creative retreat in Greece. She's paying my share. I couldn't possibly afford it."

"The wedding itself sounds really special. A whole day of drinking in an exclusive hotel. I'm looking forward to it already."

"You earned your invitation. If you hadn't badgered Dad to propose to Dee, there wouldn't be a party at all," Amy said.

"Why did they invite Marty, though? I can't believe your dad has a soft spot for him."

Amy shrugged. "They're drinking buddies. I'm sure Marty will just use the occasion to network. Dee's asked her business friends along, so he'll be in good company."

If Marty found more customers at the wedding, it wouldn't do her any harm, Kat thought. Some of them might even buy Starshine. It was exciting to be making commercial quantities at last, but work as a solo distiller was proving to be exhausting. "Thanks for suggesting this weekend away," she said. "I really need a break, especially in Cocktail Central."

"No Snow Mountain or Starshine here, though," Amy said, sipping a Cosmopolitan. "I'll have to speak to your Tim."

"I don't suppose the bar's exclusive enough," Kat said, although looking at the hipster clientele and spotlit spirits bottles, she questioned herself.

Amy pulled a face. "It's a super-smart venue," she said. "Don't forget, I've been marketing Snow Mountain for nearly a year now. There's plenty of money here." She gestured to the hipsters. "The bar staff could easily upsell to premium vodka and pricier cocktails."

Kat looked at her in mock horror. "Not until I've bought the next round, Amy. I hear too much of this talk from Tim; he never switches off either when we go out. Anyway, Marty hasn't got any Snow Mountain to sell at the moment, has he?"

It was Amy's turn to look shocked. "How did you know?"

"How do you think?" Kat asked. "Actually, it wasn't pillow talk. Tim didn't tell me anything about that dirty little secret, but Marty did. Don't forget, Marty's my partner and investor in Starshine vodka. It's thanks to him that I have a licence, premises, equipment and a brand. He didn't hesitate to remind me of that when he asked me to make Snow Mountain for him."

34

Amy gawped at her. "How can you? It comes from Bazakistan."

"Exactly. And it's a grain spirit, whereas Starshine is made from potatoes. But even without the snow-capped peaks, rolling fields and pure water of Bazakistan, I could produce a passable replica of Snow Mountain. I have my father's talent for making vodka, and Marty knows it."

"So?" Amy asked, her voice eager. "Will you do it?"

Kat shook her head. "No. Marty's angry with me, but I can't. My distillery is very small. I can't supply all the quantities he needs, and I'd need time to experiment with the recipe anyway. I'd have to put my production of Starshine, and all my plans for it, on hold to resolve his supply issue. And how would he explain that Snow Mountain was coming from the West Midlands rather than the plains of Bazakistan?"

"He'd say it was my job to do that," Amy replied. "And I could, if I had to. Something like: we're modernising the brand and it's time Snow Mountain joined the twenty-first century. Sounds plausible, doesn't it? I'm the vodka marketing manager, after all. I wish Tim would remember it, too."

Kat couldn't hide her surprise at the news of workplace friction. "I thought you and Tim got on."

Amy didn't even have the grace to look embarrassed. "He's always interfering, telling me what to do. I spent three years studying for a marketing degree, so I know what I'm talking about. Tim didn't even go to uni."

Amy must have had too many cocktails already. Perhaps they went to her head because she was so thin. Even if it was the Cosmopolitans talking, Kat couldn't let the comment pass unchallenged. "Tim could have gone to university, but Marty made him join the business. He'll own it one day, so it's only natural he wants to stay involved."

"There won't be a business if Marty can't sort out his Snow Mountain supply," Amy said. "Erik's worried he'll have to stop his cancer research, because Marty can't fund it anymore. I wish you hadn't turned him down."

Kat was beginning to regret it too. Marty hadn't helped his cause by taking such a heavy-handed approach, but she could only guess how much pride it had cost him to ask. He'd as good as told her that his livelihood was in danger, and now Amy was saying it too. What would happen if he couldn't afford to support her infant brand?

35

"I'll get more drinks," Amy said. "Same again?"

"Oh, absolutely," Kat said. She really needed another. If Amy ended up legless, too bad.

She was still lost in thought, trying to work out who she could contact for finance apart from Marty, when Amy returned from the bar.

"House special this time," Amy said. "It's sparkling, like us. And this is Ben."

The stranger brushed a floppy brown fringe out of his face. He looked to be in his mid-twenties, about their age. "Hi," he said.

He had pleasant, open features, but there was something about his eyes that triggered a subconscious alert. Kat flashed a warning glance at Amy.

Disconcertingly, Ben noticed. He must have quick reactions. "Hey, I'm not hitting on you," he said, his London accent friendly. "I literally bumped into your friend – to Amy – and the least I could do to say sorry was to buy you girls a drink."

While he seemed friendly, Kat still felt edgy.

Ben continued. "Seriously, I'm not out on the pull. I've been practising eSports at the café down the road and I came here to meet a friend. There he is now."

Kat was about to say: good, because she and Amy both had boyfriends, and what were eSports anyway? The words died on her lips, as she turned her gaze towards the door.

She recognised Vince straight away. He was the barman in the illegal casino where she'd once, foolishly, worked for Shaun Halloran. Old before his time with his trimmed ginger beard and dandyish clothes, Vince had mixed cocktails and kept order. She was sure he had convictions for violence.

Was this a trap? Shaun wanted her dead. He'd followed her from London to Birmingham, and tried to shoot her. Even from a prison cell, he'd stalked her, sending poison pen letters. She thought she'd escaped by moving house, but somehow, Shaun must have tracked her down.

Her hand gripped her bag and she pulled her foot back, ready to stand and run.

Chapter 8.   Vince

"Ben, get outside now." Vince Mowatt was in no mood for social niceties. It was bad enough having to work with Jon Halloran's good-for-nothing elder brother. The last thing he'd expected to find was the lad nattering to Kat.

"Why?" Ben said, a bewildered look on his stupid, naïve face. He obeyed, though, leaving his unfinished pint and following Vince into Hoxton Square.

"That sly bitch put your father away," Vince said.

Ben's jaw dropped. "Amy?" he said. "Or the other one?"

"You didn't even know her name?" Vince said, in disbelief. "That blonde bitch is Kat. She handed your dad over to the filth."

Her evidence had sent Shaun Halloran to prison for life, and he wanted her blood. More than that, though, Shaun craved freedom. For this reason alone, Vince sought Ben's company.

If Vince had been asked why he cared about the Hallorans, he would have said he was loyal to his friends. As a child, he'd wanted for nothing until his father, an armed robber, had died in a police shoot-out. Shaun Halloran was one of the few who had stood by Vince and his mother then, almost treating them as family. They'd been given work: shoplifting and cheque fraud for her, minding and drug-running for him.

Tall, muscular and gym-honed, Vince had mostly stayed under police radar except for a GBH conviction after an argument in a pub. He'd tried to keep his temper in check since then.

He'd never admit to anyone, especially Shaun, where his real allegiance lay: with Jonathan Halloran, only eighteen, who had calmly murdered a man in front of him.

Ben Halloran knew nothing of his younger brother's business, or of Vince's infatuation with him. The kind of nerd Vince avoided if possible, Ben was eager to kill zombies in his virtual universe, but he'd always shunned real life criminal activities. His parentage might have been called into question, had he not inherited the Halloran eyes, light blue and fringed with long lashes. Disturbingly like Jon's, they stared in shock at Vince now.

"Keep it zipped, and keep away from her," Vince warned.

"I wasn't hitting on her," Ben protested. "I hang out with girls who like eSports. It's easier that way. I just got talking to the redhead, Amy, at the bar. There was time to kill while I waited for you."

"Forget it," Vince said, still convinced Ben had fancied his chances. He looked over his shoulder. No one had followed them. "Have you got your motor with you? Let's go somewhere else. It's beer o'clock."

"We'll go back to mine," Ben said. "I've got beers in. Fancy playing GTA?"

Vince stopped bristling, even though he knew Ben would win. The lad always did. He was greased lightning on a games console. "Yeah, let's go," he said.

Ben's black Golf GTi was parked nearby. It was a handsome car: a one-off edition fitted with red leather seats, manufactured specially as a competition prize. Ben drove expertly towards his flat just north of Oxford Street. Despite leaving the satnav switched off, he seemed to find all the backstreets through which traffic flowed freely. At no time did he exceed the speed limit, Vince noted.

Ben used a magnetic card to access the garage in the basement below the flats where he lived, a privately-built low-rise block constructed of chocolate-coloured bricks perhaps forty years before. The same card allowed him to enter a lift to the second floor.

The common areas of the building were spotless. Vince was irritated, although unsurprised, to see Ben's flat cluttered with piles of computer magazines and unwashed dishes. In his own cramped bedsit, above a bookie in Tottenham, he couldn't rest unless his possessions were clean and ordered.

"You need to tidy this heap up," he told Ben. "Now."

Ben looked mutinous. "Are you threatening me?" he complained, stretching to his full stature.

They were the same height, but not evenly matched. Ben was skinny. The only muscles he'd developed were those required for a keyboard.

"I can't make plans in a pigsty," Vince snapped.

"Your problem," Ben said. "Have a beer and chill."

Tempted to take a swing at him, Vince remembered just in time that he needed to keep Ben on-side. Huffing, he gathered dirty mugs and plates from the lounge and piled them in the kitchen sink.

"There's a dishwasher," Ben grumbled.

"I suppose it'll be full," Vince said, seeing his words realised as he opened the machine. "Here, can you at least put these away?"

Ben had an expensive flat; his rent must be ten times what Vince was paying. How could he live like this?

With the dishwasher reloaded, Vince helped himself to a fridge-cold can of lager. "Stella? That'll have to do," he said. "Let's get down to business." He lounged on the brown leather sofa, freshly cleared of detritus. In front of him was the imposing screen, half the height of the room, on which they had played Grand Theft Auto with Jon only a couple of months before.

Ben misunderstood. "Here," he said, handing over a games controller.

"Later," Vince snapped. "I want to talk about your dad. You saw him last week, right?"

"Yes. I visited him in Belmarsh." The Halloran eyes were serious.

"He's had enough of prison," Vince said.

Ben nodded. "Dad asked me to help," he said slowly.

"You will, won't you?" Vince asked, suddenly anxious. He needed Ben's cash, and perhaps his computer skills too.

"I'll do whatever it takes," Ben said. "Each time I see him, he looks older and more stressed. Belmarsh is no place for a man of his age. Next year, he'll be fifty."

Vince relaxed at this proof that Ben's blood was thicker than water. "What did he want from you?"

"Only money." Ben looked away. "He said now Jon's inside too, the rest is down to you. Transport, passports, the lot."

"Does he have a plan yet?"

"That's the only piece missing."

Chapter 9.   Shaun

Increasingly, Shaun Halloran dreaded Sunday afternoons. The morning was pleasant enough: he was released from his prison wing cleaning duties, and met his fellow wing bosses in the Boardroom, or the chapel, to use its official name.

His son, Jon, was by far the youngest of the group. Pushing fifty, and looking it now that his No 3 cut had greyed, Shaun was the oldest. Still, at least he'd kept his teeth and hair. Many lags didn't. Shaun's cellmate, Sidey Carr, more than a decade younger, had a bald spot on his head and a gap in his grin.

Sidey, another churchgoer, sang hymns with the rest of the congregation as Belmarsh's alpha males agreed an increase in the price of recreational drugs. Availability was reduced after a determined effort by the authorities to search as many cells as possible. Shaun had been tipped off, so his supply line was unscathed; the price hike suited him well.

Lunch was acceptable too. The servers curried favour with an extra helping of chicken, which Shaun relished even though the roast meat was merely cheap, greasy drumsticks.

Once the door banged shut at noon, however, the hours stretched ahead, long and boring. The lags would be locked in their cells until the following morning. There were no prison officers around to take inmates to the gym, or supervise an evening association period: the wing was short-staffed again.

Staring at the unappetising sandwich he was expected to eat later, Shaun rolled a cigarette and sat on his bunk. He would have done Sidey the courtesy of standing by an open window had his cellmate been a non-smoker, but luckily, the other man liked his burn too.

Sidey, about to switch on the TV, stared at him, removing his own tobacco pouch from a trouser pocket. "Time for a post-luncheon cigar."

The skimpy roll-up was as far removed from a fat Cuban number as Shaun could imagine. Sidey disposed of it in a few deep drags. "Would you read a letter for me, Al?" he asked.

Just as Graeme Carr answered to Sidey, Shaun had his own nickname in Belmarsh: the East London abbreviation of Halloran. "Hand it over," he told Sidey.

Shaun didn't despise Sidey for his illiteracy; it was common enough in this place, possibly because it limited career options so much. Unable to read, Sidey Carr had worked as a scaffolder, then a cat burglar. It meant he could choose shorter hours and better weather. Sadly, he'd probably need a new job when he was released: his skinny frame was filling out thanks to Belmarsh's menu.

There were just two pages, written with a blue ballpoint in a childish, rounded hand. It was clear enough. "It's from your Tara," Shaun said.

Sidey nodded. "My eldest," he said. "Nineteen."

"I thought you were only thirty-six," Shaun said. True, Sidey hadn't aged well. Not only was his dark hair thinning, but his skin was leathery under the gaudy tattoos that decorated it.

"We started young," Sidey told him.

"Well, let's see what she's up to," Shaun said, making a pretence of enthusiasm. "Dear Dad, I hope you are well. Look out for me on TV on Sunday, because there's a programme about vodka and they shot film of me mixing cocktails."

"She works in the West End," Sidey said with pride. "One of those exclusive gentlemen's clubs."

Shaun raised a quizzical eyebrow. In his book, a gentlemen's club meant lap-dancing. "Sunday's today," he said, somewhat unnecessarily. "We might have missed it. She doesn't say what time, or channel, or anything."

"I'll try all of them," Sidey said, switching on the small television set for which they paid a pound a week from their paltry prison wages.

"Okay, I'll read the rest of it," Shaun said. "My word." He whistled.

"What?" Sidey asked, mid-channel change.

"You didn't say Tara batted for the other side. She's got a new partner, Danielle. Sounds like a nice girl." Shaun sniggered.

Sidey looked sheepish. "I didn't think she'd put in her life story," he said. "Anyway, so what? Your Jon's gay and all."

Shaun's eyes narrowed. He felt heat rise, almost catching in his throat. "What are you talking about?" he spluttered.

"Everyone knows," Sidey said. "I can't remember who told me. It was on the out, not here. Lesley Mowatt probably said."

"How is Lesley the expert on my son's sex life?" Shaun asked. He couldn't think when Vince's mother would have seen Jon recently, anyway.

Shaun felt sick. "Her Vince is bent as a three bob watch," he said. "That's her problem, but I won't have her spreading lies about my lad.

41

She'd better wind her neck in, and that goes for you too. And if you hear a sniff from anyone else, get them to tell me to my face."

"Why does it matter?" Sidey asked, adding, "Smell the coffee, Al. Jon and Vince lived together."

"They shared a flat, not a bed," Shaun said. "Jon had a girlfriend, although she was a skaghead. He dumped her, and not before time. Anyway, who do you think you're talking to?"

Sidey looked away, sulking. He fiddled with the television. Ten minutes passed before he seemed to remember his place in the pecking order. "Would you like a cuppa, Al?"

Shaun accepted his tribute, a black instant coffee, with a curt nod. He had a thumping headache, but none of the quack's aspirin was left. Sipping the hot drink, he tried to ignore the images that were torturing him. He wouldn't see Jon again for a week, on their next trip to the chapel. Then he'd know. He'd merely have to look into his son's eyes.

The coffee set him on edge even more, not that he'd drop a hint of it to Sidey. He couldn't show weakness. Instead, he busied his fingers with another roll-up. Smoking eased the pain coursing through his temples, giving him space to think. He couldn't afford to go crazy, or turn to drugs like his customers; he had to focus on his escape plan. For that, he needed Vince. His lip curled as he imagined what he'd do to Vince once the young man's usefulness was past.

If only he hadn't ended up inside in the first place. He'd still have the mansion in Wanstead, the criminal empire, the luxury of time to guide Jon in his personal life and train him in the business. Ben was a lost cause, but Jon would have been a worthy successor to his father.

Instead, Jon had been reduced to living above a chicken shop with Vince, and taking risks in his quest to spring Shaun from Fortress Belmarsh. Now Jon was inside too. It was all Kat's fault: she'd begun the trail that had led to Shaun's arrest.

"Here," Sidey said. "It's Tara's programme."

Shaun turned his gaze to the television, barely concealing his lack of interest.

A blonde woman's face and torso filled the tiny screen.

"Kat?" Shaun said, hardly able to utter the word.

Sidey leered, his eyes fixed on the blonde's cleavage. "It's some Russian bird who makes vodka. Mint, isn't she? I'd give her one."

Shaun saw that the woman was indeed speaking in Russian, with subtitles. "We've been producing Snow Mountain vodka in Bazakistan for over two decades," he read aloud.

Of course, it wasn't Kat, but that just proved he needed to get out. "You know," he said to Sidey, "I tried to buy some of that once, and couldn't get hold of it."

The distributor, Marty Bridges, had refused to sell him Snow Mountain for his casino. Shaun wished that he'd set fire to Marty's properties, as he'd considered doing, including the redbrick building in Birmingham's Jewellery Quarter where Kat had once lived.

He would dearly love to have her address now. It was impossible to avenge himself without knowing where she was.

"Tara does promotions for Snow Mountain," Sidey said.

"In that case," Shaun said, "can she do a favour for me? I want to find a bitch called Kat White. She's friends with the Snow Mountain distributor."

It was unusual for those who knew Shaun to decline his requests, but Sidey pushed it. "What's it worth?" the cat burglar asked.

"All the burn you can smoke," Shaun replied.

Sidey grinned. "It's a deal."

The programme continued for twenty minutes, during which Tara appeared for a split-second, brandishing a cocktail shaker.

"How come an ugly mug like you has a daughter like that? She's class," Shaun commented, his humour almost restored.

Sidey laughed. "Got lucky with my missus," he said.

Shaun was overcome by jealousy. Had his wife been alive, he'd have boasted about her too. The headache returned with such force that he was compelled to reach for his tobacco again. Then, he sat silently on his bunk, imagining he was alone with Kat, a knife in his hand.

Chapter 10.   Vince

While Vince drew the line at shaving his beard, he'd hidden his ginger hair under a flat cap and donned sunglasses. He didn't want to be recognised by anyone except Ed Rothery. The risk was real, albeit small because Ed favoured pubs south of the river, away from Vince's territory. This one had a large beer garden, where Vince had found a corner private enough to talk freely.

"What's this?" Ed demanded, craggy face scowling beneath a sandy thatch. His dirty fingernails tapped the smallest of the three pocket-sized packages Vince had given him.

"That one's your money," Vince said. "Go to the gents and count it if you like. Where the others are concerned, it's none of your business. You're just the delivery boy. I know what's in there and so does our mutual friend. He'll tell me if there's a problem."

"I don't know why he would trust you, or why I should," Ed grumbled, a whiff of sweat wafting from his armpits, his mean blue eyes staring straight into Vince's.

"You've no reason to say that, Ed." Vince was losing patience. It irked him to spend time with someone like Ed Rothery. The prison officer had a contemptible job, questionable personal hygiene, and a bad attitude.

Ed thought he was hard, with his bouncer's physique and power over Belmarsh's pitiful inmates. It was time to teach him a lesson.

"That Halstow Primary is a good school, isn't it?" Vince said, his tone conversational.

"So?" Ed wrinkled his face. If anything, it improved his looks.

"So, your Emily goes there, doesn't she?" Vince said. "Such a pretty little thing. I'd hate to see anything happen to her, if you get my meaning."

Finally, Ed did. He reddened, cursed and spat. "Back off. Touch her, and you're dead."

Vince yawned. "Really? Don't forget who you're talking to, and who my friends are. But there's no reason for us to fall out, is there? Go on, count that cash and cheer yourself up."

He could best Ed any time. His body rippled with muscles under his crisp white shirt, and he was three inches taller. Whistling to hide his irritation, he rolled a cigarette while the prison officer did as he was bid.

Vince needed the sweet taste of Golden Virginia to calm himself. Ed's surliness was the least of his worries.

Shaun had called him earlier. Landline access was controlled and monitored in Belmarsh, and mobile phones forbidden altogether, but Shaun could always access them. He'd left Vince in no doubt that Jon was off limits.

Vince had laughed it off, saying he had a lover, so why would he be interested in Shaun's son?

It wasn't Shaun's only message, though. The words echoed in Vince's head: tell your mum to zip her lip, or else. That was harder to address. She was rarely sober enough for a serious conversation. Did she really know about Jon? Vince hadn't told her. Half the time, she was too drunk to know what she was saying.

Vince decided he'd visit her after seeing Ed. Finally, he'd relax later with Pino. They'd planned an evening of sex and drugs. Jon couldn't expect fidelity, when he'd rarely slept with Vince anyway and he'd still be in prison for years.

The arrangement with Jon barely counted as a relationship, with Jon having girlfriends too and calling himself straight. Vince wanted more, of course, but he'd have to be careful now. You crossed Shaun Halloran at your peril. He was serving life because he'd shot a traitor dead. Ignoring him amounted to a suicide note.

Young Jon was no less ruthless than his father. Vince thought of Jerry and Scott, Shaun's old schoolfriends, who Jon called the bootleg boys. They'd been thinking of going freelance. Once Jon had involved them in killing a dope farmer who had tried to do just that, there had been no further talk of it. Instead, when the bootleggers branched out from booze to people smuggling, a percentage of their profits found their way to the Hallorans.

They hadn't made it big by playing nice. Just like Ed Rothery, Vince must never forget who owned him.

Chapter 11.   Marty

Marty's desk phone rang just as he'd seen the forbidding size of his overdraft. He answered once he saw it was Tanya.

"I have Marina Aliyeva on the line," she said. "Do you want to speak to her?"

"I've got nothing to say, bab, but if it'll keep her off your back…"

Tanya put the call through.

"Marty! How are you? I am so sorry about our little supply issue." Marina's tone was a great deal more conciliatory than their last conversation.

"It's not a 'little supply issue', it's a deal-breaker," Marty said. "You've seen my email, I'm sure. I won't buy from you again."

Marina's voice remained sickly-sweet. "The problem's fixed. I'm not charging you for any consignments since you identified it."

"Good, because I rejected them all. Anyway, what do you mean by 'the problem's fixed'?"

"It was our quality inspector. She admitted everything to the police."

"What kind of pressure did they apply?" He didn't suppose the Bazaki police had been kind. "Never mind, it's nothing to do with me. If toxic vodka has slipped through your processes once, it could happen again. I can't take that risk."

"No one else can make Snow Mountain," Marina said. She was beginning to sound strained.

"Want to bet?" Marty said. "I can have it made anywhere. I own the brand rights, remember?"

"You acquired them from my first husband by sleight of hand." She was snapping now. "I'm going to court to get them back."

"I'll see you there," Marty said, before the line went dead.

He might have won the argument, but it was a hollow victory. With the August bank holiday looming, he had orders for Snow Mountain, but no stock. Without Kat's co-operation, there was only one way he could satisfy his customers and improve cash flow. He asked Tanya to summon Tim, Dan and Amy to his office.

"We've got a problem, as you know," he said. "We don't have any Snow Mountain left, and our customers want more."

Tim ran a hand through his waxed fair hair. "Let me talk to Kat," he said. "She'll make it for you if she's approached right."

Marty chortled, despite the gravity of the situation. "I'm sure you'll be very persuasive, son, and I don't doubt that Kat can copy the recipe. Unfortunately, there's no time. We need to satisfy the orders this weekend. That's why I want Dan to take our entire stock of Starshine vodka and relabel it as Snow Mountain UK."

Tim almost jumped out of his seat. "No way will Kat agree to that. It's a different brand, different mouth feel..."

"Different bottles," Dan interrupted. "The Starshine design is etched, and we use glass stoppers."

Marty had expected objections. "Starshine is superior to Snow Mountain, so our customers will be getting a better product. And if we call it Snow Mountain UK, they won't expect the bottles to look the same."

"But it's better if they do," Amy said. "Marty, I can't produce and implement a marketing campaign for a Snow Mountain variant in a matter of hours. It takes months."

"Well said," Tim agreed.

Amy shot him a grateful glance.

"Do we have to do this?" Tim said. "I know sales are down because of the stock-out, but they'll pick up once Kat's making Snow Mountain for us."

"We're nearly on the overdraft limit," Marty said. It was an uncomfortable situation. He was used to the business generating more cash than he needed. Now, he was forced to sell investments and borrow to pay his wage bill.

"I'll talk Kat round, as long as you don't do anything silly," Tim said. "Meanwhile, I'll ring our biggest customers to convince them to try Starshine. How much have we got, Dan?"

"I'll get back to you," Dan said. "I don't know how we'll deliver it, though. I haven't booked drivers yet and you can't get them at short notice on a bank holiday."

"We'll have to do it ourselves," Marty said. "Hang on, what about Hero Couriers, opposite? They're pretty nippy, and they owe me a favour. I'll ask Hajji."

Outside, a few spots of rain were falling. The sound of a police siren cut through the still air. Blue lights blazing, a patrol car rounded the corner into Florence Street and screeched to a halt next to Marty. An officer wound down the window.

"You have to leave this area, Sir," the man said. "We're evacuating Florence Street."

"Sorry?" Marty asked.

"It's a terrorist incident." The policeman pointed to the Hero Couriers garage.

"A bomb?" Marty asked, incredulous.

The officer's eyes wavered. "I can't tell you anything more, but you have to leave," he said.

"This is my company." Marty gestured to his premises. "We've got flammable vodka in that warehouse. I'll get the workforce out as soon as possible." He couldn't afford to waste time. Hero was so close, an explosion would be devastating.

Another patrol car blocked the entrance to the main road. "He'll move for you," the officer yelled, as Marty sprinted back inside. "He's just stopping traffic coming in."

Marty unlocked the inner door to the lobby. If the worst happened and Florence Street went up in flames, how would his business ever recover? His insurance policy might cover his depleted stock, but he'd be sued if he didn't supply customers and pay his staff.

Despite his financial woes, it was the risk to his employees that sent him rushing into the building. "Tanya," he bellowed, "tell everyone to get out, fast. There's a bomb. I'm taking you all to the pub, and it's on my credit card."

Chapter 12. Shaun

It was eight o'clock: the end of the inmates' evening association period. Shaun and Sidey had returned to their cell. Shaun knew, as soon as he heard the tuneless whistling, that Ed Rothery was the officer locking them in for the night.

"I've got a delivery for you, Halloran," Rothery said, poking his unlovely sandy head around the door.

No doubt the screw intended the frisson of alarm that assailed Shaun for a few seconds. Ed Rothery often brought small parcels for him, but they were never given to him direct.

Rothery handed over a letter, smirking as Shaun inhaled with a gasp.

"Thanks," Shaun said. The sandy-haired man should remember who was paying him. They'd have words tomorrow.

"Don't mention it," the officer said, his bouncer-like physique looming over the two cons and making the cell feel even more crowded than usual. "It's from your girlfriend. Sweet dreams." He marched out, the door banging shut after him.

"Girlfriend, Al?" Carr asked.

"Penfriend, Sidey," Shaun corrected him. "A sex-starved nurse."

Sidey Carr licked his lips. "You should ask for a conjugal visit."

"Where do you think we are? Sweden?" Shaun asked. "No, don't tell me. Watch telly, or something. I want to read Tracy's news in peace."

He looked forward to her letters more than he cared to admit. Tracy, who apparently wrote to several prisoners, always saw her glass as half-full. That was stupid of her, but it entertained him. Although they'd never met, he heard her voice chirruping from the page.

'We had a triple bypass operation to perform today,' he read. 'As soon as he was up and about, the patient was asking for a burger and fries, according to my friend Teresa. A burger and fries!!! What was he thinking?'

Tracy hadn't answered the rhetorical question. Instead, she told him that this had been a good week for her; she had breakfasted on Slimfast shakes for three days running without reaching for a mid-morning Mars Bar. With luck, she would lose a pound. That would make Teresa jealous: the pair had trained as nurses together many decades ago, and both had steadily added weight since then. Now in their early fifties, their own employer, the NHS, had chided them for their obesity. Tracy was on a mission to drop to a size 16 by Christmas.

She signed off by saying that was enough about her, but how was Shaun?

He chuckled, without mirth. What did she think? He was stuck in a whitewashed box with Sidey Carr, who had just used their shared toilet. The unpleasant aroma elicited a curse from Shaun.

Sidey grinned. "Sorry, Al. Had the curry earlier."

"And don't I know it," Shaun grumbled. "Instant weight loss. You need it, though."

The threads of a plan that had been forming in his mind began to knit together. There was no point waiting for Ben to liberate him. The lad's head was in the clouds.

Tracy had unwittingly given Shaun inspiration. His penfriend's troubles resulted from one simple fact: her calorie intake generally exceeded the calories she used. There was no magic diet, no superfood or brand that could fix that. Unlike Sidey, who was already suffering the consequences of prison stodge only a month into his sentence, Shaun had been careful to keep himself trim as soon as he'd been sent inside. He'd watched what he ate and worked out in the prison gym.

Jon did the same. In the brief week when they'd shared a cell, Shaun had explained his survival philosophy to Jon. The boy didn't really need telling. He was already lord of his wing, as Shaun was of his: controlling the distribution and sale of drugs and mobile phones with the help of tools like Ed Rothery.

Tracy could be his instrument too. If Shaun lost weight, perhaps while faking other symptoms, he could play her like a violin. All he need do was persuade her to lobby for his transfer to a hospital outside the prison. Nobody had ever escaped from Belmarsh. Jon had tried to spring Shaun, and now he was inside with him. In a hospital, by contrast, security would be weaker. Shaun's guile, Ben's money and Vince's muscle could overcome it.

He needed first to ensure that Tracy trusted him. It was rare for Shaun to open his heart, but this time, he had to do it. He sat at the small table in the cell with a pencil and notebook, ready to craft a reply to his new friend.

'Dear Tracy,' he wrote. 'It is a tonic to hear from a lovely girl like yourself. I have never had female friends except my dear, late wife. I miss her and dream about her every night.'

It was true, after a fashion. Meg's death from cancer five years before had left him floundering. He wouldn't have become obsessed by Kat, or taken the risks that had sent him behind bars, if his wife were still alive. Now, she appeared to him as he drifted to sleep each evening, sometimes flitting through the fantasies of night as well. He took comfort from her shadowy presence.

Meg could still shine brightly in his memories, but Tracy must be the object of his worship – or, at least, believe she was. Shaun smiled, and signed the letter with love.

Chapter 13.   Kat

"Breakfast at the Mailbox?" Tim suggested, opening the passenger door of his sporty Subaru for Kat.

"Sure. Let's treat ourselves, because today's the day I'm getting a pay rise."

While the small amount Marty had offered before hadn't materialised, Kat was confident she'd secure a large increase during their meeting later that morning. After all, he really needed her help to keep his business afloat.

Traffic on the short journey from Edgbaston was lighter than usual for eight o'clock. The schools' autumn term hadn't started yet. Many workers used the bank holiday earlier in the week as an excuse for an extended break. Tim took only ten minutes to drive to East West Bridges.

"Look, I'm the first one in." He parked on the tarmac.

"Was there really a bomb there?" Kat asked, pointing at Hero Couriers' shuttered premises across the road. It seemed incredible in such a sleepy backwater.

Tim looked sombre. "It must have been defused, or we'd have been blown sky-high. It doesn't get more exciting in Florence Street."

He reached for her hand. "Let's get that breakfast."

They walked to the Mailbox, an upmarket complex of shops and bars, and found an outside table overlooking a canal.

"Coffee for me," Kat said, "and eggs royale, with smoked salmon. Did your dad really say Starshine vodka was better than Snow Mountain?"

"Yes, he did."

"Then I'll have a glass of champagne as well."

A boat chugged past below, its bright red sides sending reflections rippling through the water.

"Maybe one day I'll live on a houseboat," Kat said, "travelling through the city as the fancy takes me."

"Enough daydreaming," Tim said. "Are you a hundred per cent happy about making Snow Mountain for Dad?"

"If he pays me enough," Kat said. She raised her glass. "A toast to pay rises!"

"A toast to toast," Tim said, tackling the full English breakfast set before him.

Fortified by fizz and caffeine, she strolled back with Tim for their nine thirty meeting.

Although they were a few minutes early, Amy and Marty were already waiting for them in his office. The coffee tray was on the table.

"Can you pour the drinks, please, bab?" Marty asked Amy.

She gave him a look that said, 'I'm not your PA,' but nonetheless obliged. At least she knew that Kat took her caffeine strong and dark.

Marty passed around a generous plate of shortbread fingers. He and Tim both helped themselves.

"So," Marty said, oozing bonhomie, "you can make Snow Mountain vodka for us."

"Yes," Kat said. "No one will be able to tell the difference. I'll need extra kit, and time to experiment, as we discussed."

"How long?" Marty asked.

"Three weeks minimum after the equipment's installed."

"Then I'll buy it ASAP," Marty said. He frowned. "As soon as we're done here, I'll talk to the bank about upping the overdraft limit. Somehow, I'll get the cash together."

"Could you sell property?" Tim asked.

"Leave that one with me, Tim. It's not your concern," Marty said. "Your job is sweet-talking the customers into waiting."

"I can do that." Tim grinned. "I'll offer them Starshine at a good price to bridge the gap."

Kat's eyes narrowed. "You're bearing that discount, I take it?" she told Marty. "It shouldn't come out of my profit share."

"Yes, all right."

He agreed so quickly that she was sure she had the upper hand.

"It's a much better idea than relabelling Starshine bottles as Snow Mountain," Amy said.

"That would be crazy. Who on earth would do that?" Kat said.

Did a glance pass between Marty and Tim? She couldn't be certain.

"So, Amy," Marty said, "how are we going to market Snow Mountain UK?"

"It's the 21st century," Amy said. "That demands a fresh new approach to life, and to vodka."

"Great." Tim's eyes were shining. "Birmingham's on the up, especially with millennials. We'll capitalise on the city's space age image, the shiny new buildings and the clubbing scene."

"That might work for Starshine, but it isn't right for Snow Mountain," Amy said. "London's the place for high end gin and craft beers, and that's where Snow Mountain UK should be based. Kat, you'll have to move production there."

Tim's lips tightened. His father, too, was simmering.

Marty came to the boil. "Do you want costs to double? I need to save money, not pour it down the drain," he said. "Kat, you can fit the new kit in your existing space, can't you?"

Kat nodded.

"Good. That's sorted, then. Amy, you'll be working with Tim's idea. Got it?"

"Yes." Amy didn't look pleased.

"Right. Let's get started." Marty rose to his feet, evidently intent on marshalling them out of his office.

"Marty, can I have a private word, please?" Kat said.

"Of course." He was all smiles.

She waited until Tim and Amy had gone.

"About that pay rise, Marty. I'm taking on significant responsibilities, and my salary needs to reflect that. I should be paid at least double my current rate. And East West Bridges should be picking up the cost, not the Starshine joint venture."

Who was really going to benefit from her hard work? It was time to negotiate, and she wasn't underselling herself.

Chapter 14.   Vince

Vince was wearing his flat cap and sunglasses again, although summer was over. Just a month ago, it had been light at 6am. Vince had seen the sun rise, gold illuminating the quiet trees, as he jogged with Pino through the southern tip of Epping Forest. Pino had insisted they run here as dawn broke, a gesture that had seemed as romantic as the rosy sky.

In late September, the woods felt different: cloaked in darkness, and chilly. Vince shivered. In his hi-vis jacket, he could have been a workman about to start an early shift at the hospital nearby. Later, the paths across the forest would be busy with commuters and joggers. They were deserted at this hour, as Vince had foreseen.

He was certain Pino would be here soon. The barber had told him this was his routine before breakfasting near his workplace, a hairdresser's in Leyton. Vince removed the fluorescent jerkin, folding it small and leaving it beneath undergrowth. It might make him unobtrusive to a casual observer, but he didn't want it to catch Pino's eye.

A sound, the fast, rhythmic tread of trainers, disturbed the silent air. Vince skulked in shadows. His palms began to sweat as the runner approached, his heart racing. Treacherous blood, carrying a foreign agent, pounded through his veins. Hands trembling, he shone a torch on the man running towards him.

Pino stopped at once. It was him, without a doubt. Vince had expected to feel anger, but not the desire that surged through him at the sight of Pino's hooked nose and waxed black hair.

The brown eyes that had once carried the promise of love were wide with shock. Pino would be dazzled and unable to see him. "What do you want, bro?" the runner asked.

Vince fought to utter the words he wanted to say.

Something about him, his height perhaps, spooked the other man. Pino fiddled with a pocket in his joggers, and waggled a twenty pound note at Vince. "Take it."

Vince ignored the offer, finally finding his voice. "Why, Pino?"

"Vince?" Pino stepped backwards. He didn't sound pleased to be reacquainted. "We must stop meeting like this. It was fun while it lasted, but…"

"You didn't return my calls. You blocked my messages. My letters were returned marked 'gone away'. You've moved house, haven't you?"

"Only down the road. What's it to you? I told you, Vince, it's over."

"I'll never forget you."

Pino preened. "They all say that."

"You know why I won't. Why I can't. You gave me HIV and Hep C. You knew you were positive, didn't you?"

"Get over it." Pino said. "It's not a death sentence."

"It's a life sentence," Vince said. His mouth quivered, his temples twitching. Anger began to smoulder as Pino stayed unapologetically silent. "Why can't you say sorry?"

Pino yawned. "You're such a drama queen."

Vince's rage bubbled over. There was a flick-knife in his pocket. He reached for it with his free hand. A faint glimmer of moonlight caught the blade as it opened. Vince had never killed a man before; watching Jon do it didn't count. When he considered what Jon would do now, though, he knew the answer.

Pino screamed, a yell both incredulous and despairing, and turned to flee. Vince rushed him, aiming his knife for the gap between the shoulder blades. Panting with the effort, he pulled it out, smelling blood as he did so.

Pino was still standing. He moved to face Vince once more, grappling with him.

Vince thrust the blade forward, twisting its point through his opponent's ribcage. He wanted Pino's heart. If that didn't work, he'd puncture a lung, and Pino would perish anyway.

"Help," Pino shouted. The sound echoed through the forest.

Frantically, Vince looked around. He hadn't anticipated noise or a struggle. Although he hadn't seen another soul, suppose someone heard Pino's dying cries?

"Shut up," he said, jerking the knife from his victim's chest. Fear and fury lent him adrenaline: he sliced across Pino's throat, quelling the man's voice, before slashing deeper. There was a bubbling noise and the metallic smell of blood. The hot, sticky liquid gushed out.

Vince found the yellow waistcoat, using it to dab at his face, hands and chest. Despite his anxiety, he had the presence of mind to pick up his knife and torch. Stealthily, he crept towards the ponds a few minutes' walk to the north. It felt like an eternity.

Still, he saw nobody. Throwing the knife and torch as far as he could into the depths, he plunged in after them.

The shock of the icy water was like a thrill ride, consuming all his attention and thankfully calming his panic. Vince knew it wasn't the end of a nightmare, though, but the beginning. Ever since he'd had the clinic's letter, he'd wished he could wash himself clean of each deadly virus, like the bloodstains that were vanishing in the pool.

He could never sleep with Jon again. It had only happened a few times, before Jon went inside and Vince met Pino. The younger Halloran was bi-curious at best. Why would he bother with condoms and a tainted lover when he left Belmarsh?

Whatever happened, Vince was devoted to Jon; he couldn't hurt him. He certainly couldn't put him through this: the half-life of constant medication that stretched ahead.

The memory of sex with Jon, the best that Vince had ever known, nearly made him weep. Technically, Pino was a better lay, but there was no love involved in that equation. It had been exciting enough for Vince to contemplate a relationship, though, little realising Pino would wreak his damage and move on.

Shaun must not find out: ideally about Vince's HIV-positive status, but definitely, and especially now, about the sex with Jon. Once the truth was known, Shaun would be overwhelmed by wrath. He'd have no further use for Vince.

A lifetime of medical treatment or a slow death without it was nothing to the swift and painful retribution that Shaun would exact. It would be a mistake to imagine that Shaun, in prison, was neutralised: others making that error had paid with their lives.

Dread and loss flooded Vince's spirit. He considered staying in the chilly pool until the waters overcame him. Instead, he emerged, dripping and spluttering, the sun's rays failing to warm his freezing bones as dawn began to break.

Chapter 15.   Marty

"You've had a letter that says what?" Marty asked.

"East West Bridges is using the Snow Mountain trademark illegally, and I'll be sued if I continue to sell the vodka you've supplied," Dominic Davis said, his Black Country vowels more pronounced on the phone. "It's from a lawyer acting for the Snow Mountain Company of Kireniat, Bazakistan."

"Can you email a copy, please?" Marty said. "It's a load of rubbish, Dom; you know that. We go back a long way. You've been buying from me for twenty-five years."

"You imported vodka until a couple of months ago, though, didn't you?" Dominic said. "Now you're making it down the road in Birmingham."

"We have to move with the times," Marty said, on message.

He was more worried than he wished to admit. Four months after Dan had found methanol, Marty's bank account was still in the red. He'd borrowed even more heavily to ramp up production before Christmas. Just as he'd started supplying Snow Mountain again, Marina Aliyeva seemed determined to stop him.

How many more key customers had received letters like this? He hadn't given her a list, so she must be guessing who they were.

Dominic agreed to scan the letter and email it to him. By the time their conversation finished, three new messages had arrived in his inbox, and he'd missed calls from Tim and Tanya. He could imagine what they were about.

Shrugging, Marty picked up the phone again, dialling his lawyer's number. Katherine Evans was already defending him against the lawsuit Marina had filed in her claim for the Snow Mountain brand.

"She's taking risks, isn't she?" Katherine said, once he'd explained. "We can get an injunction right now to stop her sending letters to your customers. When her claim is thrown out, which I fully expect it to be, you could sue her for losses sustained as a result of those she's sent already."

"That's if my business survives long enough to go after her," Marty said, "and if Marina has any assets left by the time I do. She hasn't found another distributor outside Bazakistan, despite her tub-thumping."

"Why's that?"

"How long have you got? First of all, the likely suspects know I own the Snow Mountain brand, although they're probably aware of her claim. If they weren't before, they will be now. Secondly, it's common knowledge that I've refused to buy from her."

"Does anyone know why?" Katherine asked.

"I've said nothing about the methanol. I don't want to be tainted by association."

"I think you should let people know," Katherine said. "Stick to the facts. They have a habit of leaking anyway. It's not my call, though. That's down to your communications people."

"That'll be Amy in marketing," Marty said. "I'll discuss it with her."

"You've no doubt got plenty of proof that her vodka was contaminated, and that you stopped it getting into the hands of drinkers because of your rigorous testing regime."

"Right."

"So, you can build a defence file and a communications strategy," Katherine said. "Any questions?"

"How do I stop Marina destroying my business?"

"We'll take out an injunction against her. I'll also give you a statement you can send your customers. It will say that, if they receive a letter from Marina's company professing rights to the Snow Mountain trademark, they should ignore it. We'd tell them her claim is entirely without merit and is being robustly defended by my firm. I can work with Amy on the words, if you like."

"Yes, please." Amy could replace the legalese with marketing spin.

"There's more you can do to reassure customers. For instance, you could offer to indemnify them in full if Marina sues them – as long as they give you sole conduct of the defence, naturally. I think it's unlikely she would sue individual customers, because any moderately competent lawyer would advise her not to. But you'd give your customers a warm and comfortable feeling, which is always a good thing in these situations."

"Fine," Marty said. "I'll do it. It's November already, and I can't afford to lose sales in the run-up to Christmas."

"Of course, before you incur legal fees, you could ring Marina and see if she'll back down."

That was so unlikely that Marty considered asking if Katherine believed in Santa Claus.

59

"It's worth a try, Marty. It doesn't cost anything. You might mention that if she continues down this road, it will almost certainly lead to complete financial ruin for her."

Another dozen emails were flashing on his screen. As soon as he'd said goodbye to Katherine, he found the one from Dominic. The pompous letter from Marina's lawyers put fire in his belly to call her.

"I've been waiting for this," Marina said. "I hope you've learned your lesson. You can't make Snow Mountain in England and get away with it."

Marty held the phone at arm's length and counted to ten. "I've told you before: I own that brand. If you carry on fighting me, the only winners are lawyers."

"Sorry," Marina said. "Vodka from England just isn't Snow Mountain. It should be distilled from pure Bazaki water and grain."

"Kat manages perfectly with Birmingham water and Warwickshire wheat."

Marina laughed. "You clearly trust my daughter to make vodka, even if you don't trust me. Send her back home. She can do the job in Bazakistan."

"As if that'll happen," Marty said. His dislike for Marina was amplified in Kat to an overwhelming hatred of her mother.

"Then start buying from me again, or your customers will vanish like frightened deer."

"No," Marty said, his patience snapping. "You're not dragging my business down with yours. Back off, Marina, or I'll tell the world you sold me vodka tainted with methanol."

It was the nuclear option. After the phone call, when he'd finally calmed down, he knew he couldn't do it. Once the brand was tainted in the public eye, who'd remember the problem arose in Bazakistan rather than Birmingham?

He could only hope Katherine's letters did the trick. Otherwise, he'd lose everything.

Chapter 16.   Vince

Vince's lock-up garage boasted a series of horizontal metal beams above his head, forming the bottom of a triangle with its apex at the roof. He'd seen films of gangland rivals suspended from meat-hooks, and in idle moments, suspected Jon would enjoy trying it. Vince had simply slung a couple of rolls of old carpet in the roof space. On top of one of these, he kept a Glock 17 pistol.

Detection meant an automatic five-year prison sentence, as poor Jon knew to his cost. The gun only received an outing on special occasions, like today. At Jon's insistence. Vince was riding shotgun with Jerry and Scott.

They had their own vehicle: a white Ford Transit van, as anonymous as his hi-vis waistcoat. Vince travelled ahead on a Honda Grom motorbike. This was black, and it didn't turn heads, except discerning ones. They were in short supply in the pub car parks he frequented with the bootleg boys.

Vince stopped at one of his favourites, close to the North Circular Road where it sliced through Walthamstow. Here, the houses were pebbledashed thirties terraces, and the pub had been constructed at the same time, in a mock Tudor roadhouse style. The parking area wrapped itself around the building. Vince chose a spot at the rear, where high walls ensured privacy from surrounding gardens. There had never been any CCTV cameras there before, and he didn't see any now.

It was a cold spot, too far from the road for the morning frost to have melted. Vince was glad of his leathers. Presently, the Transit pulled in beside him, followed swiftly by the pub landlord emerging from the back door. A shaven-headed local man in his thirties, tattooed and pierced, he looked like a younger version of Jerry and Scott, who were both heading for the big five-oh.

Jerry, balding and podgy, stepped out of the van to greet him. "All right, Gaffer?"

"What have you got for me?" Gaffer was a man of few words, and apparently no name. Jerry and Scott never called him anything else. Vince supposed that, if he was bothered, he could always read the alcohol licence sign above the front door.

"Stella, Duvel, Hoegaarden and spirits," Jerry said. "Take a look." Scott, shorter and hairier, was out of the van now and unlocking the back.

"Hmm, not much call for Hoegaarden at the moment. It's a summer drink," Gaffer said, picking over the crates in the Transit. "I'll have three crates of Stella and another of rum. You." He pointed at Vince, standing close to them in his leathers and helmet. "Help me take them in."

"Not my job," Vince replied.

"I'll do it," Scott said.

"Thought he was the muscle?" Gaffer complained.

"That's not what the muscle's here for," Jerry said, balling his hands into fists.

"I get it," Gaffer said. "Is he necessary? There's never trouble in my gaff."

"I'm the insurance," Vince said, without rancour.

Once Gaffer had his free supplies, the back door opened once more, this time for paying customers. With Christmas just a few weeks away, they did brisk business before moving to their next outlet.

Jerry was proud of their work: it was like a social service, he always said. By importing beer from Belgium, they were making life easier for ordinary drinkers. How else could anyone afford booze, given the crippling level of tax in Britain? Vince thought Jerry and Scott were making life easier for themselves, too. Still, their profits were nowhere near what they used to be, with Brexit pushing prices up on the Continent. It was lucky they'd found a way to diversify.

With Vince for protection, they didn't encounter so much as a murmur of dissent from customers, and the pistol stayed in his pocket. They'd sold out by the fifth stop on their tour.

"See you back at mine," Scott said. "I've saved beer for later."

Vince nodded. He returned to his home turf to stash away his bike and gun. There was no point taking the latter with him unless he needed it, and he wouldn't at Scott's cosy country hideaway. Paying cash, he caught a train from Tottenham Hale to Broxbourne.

Until then, he'd been too busy to brood. Vince stared out of the window at the passing scenery. However hard he tried to take an interest in his surroundings, Jon, Pino and a lifetime of prescription medicine stalked his thoughts. The fifteen-minute journey seemed longer.

As the railway slipped into the trading estates on the Tottenham Marshes, he tried to spot the industrial unit where Shaun had run an illegal casino. There, Vince had mixed cocktails for punters, his favourite job ever. It had come to an abrupt halt when Kat shopped Shaun to the police.

While the train rattled through Northumberland Park and Angel Road, Vince wondered how these dismal places had such poetic names. Industry gave way to suburbs at London's edge, but it was only past Cheshunt that the railway broke out into the countryside, hugging the path of the River Lee. Brown, feathery winter trees and still grey lakes dominated the watery landscape. His lips tightened as he remembered Epping Forest.

Eventually, he was deposited in Broxbourne, prosperous and picturesque, quite unlike the start of his journey. Scott's cottage was a ten-minute walk from the station. Vince marched past a few whitewashed twentieth century dwellings, a church and a park. A darkening sky stretched above and around him.

He understood why Scott, brought up in the East End like almost everyone he knew, had decamped to a village. Here, in his cottage with its huge garden, the bootlegger could keep secrets. It was much harder in the city, where it was wise not to rent a lock-up for too long. Rivals, policemen or simple busybodies might take an interest. Scott's cottage was pretty, too, its mellow old brick softened further by pots of pink cyclamen in front of it.

Scott, opening the door, looked every inch the country gentleman, or at any rate, a pocket-sized one. He wore a tweed jacket, blue twill shirt and chinos. "Come in," he said, a bottle of strong Belgian beer in his hand.

A dog, lean and grey, bounded forward at speed and stood next to the squat man, its brown eyes wary. "You've met Sooty before, haven't you?" Scott said.

"Yes," Vince said curtly. He'd never liked dogs, but the retired greyhound didn't spook him as much as others: it was quite reserved. It hung back, tangling itself in Scott's legs and staring at Vince.

"My family's out," Scott said, without explaining where they were. His girlfriend had teenagers, who were always being ferried to dance classes, cinema trips and sporting fixtures. Their lives were very different from Vince's experience. He had virtually brought himself up, like the other kids on his estate.

Jerry's voice boomed from the kitchen at the back. "Beer's over here."

Vince followed Scott and Sooty, taking care not to trip on the uneven flagstone floor or hit his head on the low doorway into the back. The

63

cottage had been built in days of yore for shorter people than him. Scott fitted into it comfortably.

Jerry had left the crate on the oak table in the centre of the room, and was sitting on a matching chair. He was drinking Hoegaarden, evidently without a care for the season. "Help yourself," he said.

"I'll just warm the pasties in the microwave," Scott said.

Vince raised an eyebrow.

"The vegans are away," Scott said. "Obvious, innit?"

Vince hung his Crombie overcoat on a chair, sprawled in it and opened a beer. It tasted good. Since hitting twenty-five, he'd started experiencing evil hangovers, but that wouldn't stop him drinking until the crate was empty.

Scott shoved a steaming Cornish pasty towards Vince. It was lying on a white plate with black lettering announcing TEA-TOAST-JAM around the edge.

"Is that to prove you can read?" Vince asked.

"Just eat it," Scott said, handing another to Jerry and keeping two for himself. With great affection, he fed morsels to Sooty. No longer sulking, the animal seized them as if on the point of starvation.

"Doesn't seem fair insisting the dog goes vegan," Jerry said.

"S'what I thought," Scott said, his mouth full. "Not fair on me neither, innit?" He swigged some beer. "I can't wait for my holiday. We're going next week. Barbie booked it last minute. All-inclusive package on the Costa Brava; five-star hotel. I'll eat whatever I want: steak, bacon, pizza."

"And drink," Jerry said.

"Sounds pricy," Vince said. Perhaps it was time to reduce Scott's profit share.

Scott's mean eyes glared at him. "We got it for free last time. I had all our money back. Barbie's friend knows one of those claims lawyers. We told him we had food poisoning, and bingo. Easy cash, innit?"

"I fancy a holiday in the sun myself," Jerry said.

"Can we talk about work?" Vince said, starting on his third bottle. "You won't be bringing anyone in next week if you're away."

"Week after," Jerry said. "Then booze the week after that, for the Christmas trade."

"I've got three customers," Vince said, removing one of his smartphones from a trouser pocket. "Here are the photos. That guy," he pointed to one of them, "has a passport already, so he doesn't need the full service." That was a shame, because they'd only make five grand out of him before expenses. They had no clue about the quality of the passport, either.

"Shaun got work lined up for them?" Jerry asked.

"Shaun and his friends," Vince said. One of the travellers would be despatched to Shaun's skunk farm. The others would disappear somewhere into the Hallorans' huge web of contacts. Within their prison cells, Shaun and Jon bought, sold and bartered anything that would turn a profit. That now included people. Vince had to hand it to Jerry: it had been his idea. There was more money in migrants than booze runs.

"So, we've got to find passports for this pair?" Jerry said. "They're Chinese-looking."

"And young," Vince said. "That makes it easier. Students, for instance." He paid five hundred pounds to rent a passport for a week, no questions asked. Of course, there was a risk that both immigrant and passport would disappear once in Britain, but it hadn't happened yet. He, and Shaun's friends, could be persuasive.

"I'll ask around," Jerry said. "Might go to the local casino. Always Chinese gamblers there; I bet they're keen for more cash."

"Thanks," Vince said. "While Scott's away, can you collect the guy with the passport? He's in Bruges, so you could fill the van while you're there. In December, we can sell booze like that." He snapped his fingers.

"Suppose so," Jerry muttered, his tone unenthusiastic. He yawned. "Your kitchen smells of meat pies, Scott. Barbie will be cross. I'm going to do you a favour by having a rollie."

"You will not. Go outside," Scott commanded. "You and all, Vince."

Vince was extracting the makings of a spliff from his pocket. In spite of the beer, he was on edge. It had been a long day. Once he'd assembled the giant roll-up, he donned his thick black coat and followed Jerry into the back garden.

Night had fallen. The dog streaked past, haring to dark corners unreached by the light spilling onto the patio from the kitchen. Vince and Jerry smoked companionably by the open door, standing on flagstones similar to those inside the cottage.

"Smells like strong stuff," Jerry acknowledged.

Vince grinned and grunted. He vocal chords were relaxing already, along with the rest of him.

The greyhound returned with a small bone in its mouth. Jerry recoiled. "Awrgh! I bet that's one of Anton's fingers," he said.

Vince laughed. It was the funniest thing he'd heard all week. He was chortling so much, the smoke almost choked him. Fancy Jerry recalling the dope farmer's death at the exact moment that Vince was relishing a reefer. "Don't be shilly," he said, his speech sounding unaccountably slurred, "I put him shix feet under." It had been hard work digging a grave for Anton after Jon had slashed his throat. Naturally, it was Anton's own fault; he shouldn't have tried to defraud Jon's dad, should he?

Jerry stared at him.

Vince searched the corners of his mind for a sober thought. Perhaps it hadn't been six feet: more like six inches. Still, the garden was massive, and being in the country, a wide variety of animals must have lived and died in it. It was probably full of bones. There was no reason why Sooty should have tunnelled through the soil to Anton's. He tried to enlighten Jerry. "Dogs and bones," he said. "Ish a rabbit, I 'shpect." Throwing the butt of the spliff into the darkness, he returned inside. "You tell 'im, Shcott."

"Tell him what?" Scott asked. He seemed somehow even smaller than before. "You'll have to break up the party now. I've just had a text from the Barbster. She's on her way back." He wafted his hands around the still-open back door. "How am I going to explain this?"

"Exshplain what?" Vince said, puzzled as Scott began spraying air freshener all around the kitchen.

Jerry didn't even offer a lift, which may have been just as well, as he'd had a few beers. Vince floated back to the station, the night's chill bouncing off him.

The London train was hot, stuffy and practically empty. Vince fell asleep, dreaming of Anton clawing his way out of the cold earth. About to scream, he woke to find the train was just leaving Tottenham Hale. He had to walk home up the High Road from Seven Sisters.

Chapter 17.   Kat

The Monday evening before Christmas was surprisingly quiet in Birmingham's Jewellery Quarter. Giant neon rings and chains sparkled colourfully, dangling from the attics of the old redbrick buildings that lined the area's streets. Kat, whisked past in Tim's Uber, was enchanted.

"The lights are beautiful," she told him. "But where is everyone?"

"Suffering pre-Christmas exhaustion?" he suggested. "I sold every drop of Snow Mountain you could make this month; there must be a lake of it being drunk."

"But not here," Kat pointed out. A few pubs were brightly lit, with groups of smokers outside, but most premises were shuttered and silent.

She remarked on it to Marty, when they arrived at the Italian restaurant he'd booked for his works Christmas party.

"Monday night's always slow, bab." Marty chuckled. "That's how I get a good deal for us."

A good deal for him, Kat thought sourly. It appeared to be the one night of the year when Marty treated his staff. All his businesses were represented under one roof: she was there for Starshine vodka, her brother, Erik, for Darria Enterprises, and a horde of East West Bridges employees were making merry with bottles of champagne. Marty seemed to be related to half of them.

Amy materialised at their elbow with two glasses. "Have some fizz, Kat. You can't talk to Tim and Marty all evening."

Kat allowed herself to be led away. "Marty's the last person I want to hang out with," she said.

"I guessed as much," Amy replied. "Look, just stay out of his way and get drunk. That's what everyone else does."

Kat sat with Amy and Erik as starters were served: a selection of bread, olives and cold meat on wooden boards, from which the diners helped themselves.

"You can see Tim later," Amy said. Kat's boyfriend was deep in conversation with Dan.

"If only he weren't Marty's son," Kat said.

"It could be worse," Erik said. "He'll inherit the business when Angela persuades Marty to call it a day."

"You've got it bad, haven't you?" Amy was sympathetic.

"I have," Kat confessed. "Sometimes, I imagine booking flights to Vegas and coaxing him into a wedding chapel. Then I remember that I work for his father. Marty's not quite my boss, and not quite my business partner, but he controls the purse strings."

"That's the problem with our darria initiative," Erik said. "He's in command, and he's not spending anything. I must admit, this research freeze is frustrating. I went into partnership with Marty because I thought he was more ethical than Big Pharma. But if I'd gone to the mainstream pharmaceutical companies, I'd have the funds I need."

"He just wanted to make a quick buck from your herbal tea," Kat said. "You should stick up for yourself."

"Let's forget about work tonight," Amy said. She signalled to the black-clad waiter. "Can we have a tray of vodka shots, please? Say a dozen of them?"

The drinks arrived. "We'll play a game," Amy said. "I have never, ever, slept with Tim Bridges."

Erik jolted forward in alarm. "What?"

"It's a game," Amy said. "If you've done it, you have to down a shot."

Kat took a glass.

"In one," Amy said.

Kat knocked back the clear liquid. It obviously wasn't either Starshine or Snow Mountain. "Not ours," she said.

"You must have words with the sales director," Amy said, grinning. "Your turn next."

"This is truth or dare, isn't it?" Erik asked.

"With a vengeance," Amy said.

"So, this is what they teach you at university?" Kat said.

They emptied the twelve glasses. Amy called for more.

Kat was dimly aware that Erik was plying both girls with bread in an effort to soak up the alcohol. "No carbs for me," she told him.

He looked askance at her. "You're drinking too much. Back to mine for coffee afterwards."

There was espresso after the meal, though, in a tiny white cup with an almond biscuit next to it. Marty, hopping between each table, insisted on ordering one for each of them. "It'll improve your singing voices," he told them. "We're going to a karaoke bar next."

"Who arranged that?" Erik asked.

"Tanya's idea," Marty said. "She's word-perfect on Duran Duran, and so am I."

Kat looked longingly at Tim. Was there any way to escape the eighties revival and return to her flat with him?

Amy noticed. "Tim should come here more often," she told Marty. "They don't stock our brands."

"I know," Marty said. "I've got nothing to sell them, though. Kat can't make Snow Mountain fast enough." He looked more sober than anyone else, although he'd been drinking champagne as if it were lemonade.

"I didn't even make Starshine this month. I had to switch all production over to Snow Mountain," Kat said. As she'd feared, her new craft brand was suffering, its sales grinding to a halt almost as soon as they began. She had to tackle Marty about it, but now was not the time.

"Don't I know it? We're leaving money on the table," Marty said. "The unit I gave you is too small."

"Have you got somewhere bigger for me?" Kat asked.

"Not yet," Marty said. "We should move you to a larger place on the outskirts of Brum, a purpose-built facility even. Then I'd transfer the warehouse from Florence Street. That building has had its day. The bomb scare in August was the last straw. I'm minded to apply for planning permission for a hotel, like the one they stuck around the corner. The area isn't what it used to be. There are student flats popping up, and all the boozers are becoming gastropubs. I may as well cash in."

His eyes were twinkling now, probably at the prospect of money rather than any Christmas spirit. "I wouldn't build a hotel, just sell the site to Hilton or the Holiday Inn. You can walk there from the station. It's a thought."

Tanya, a sprig of mistletoe pinned to her crimson-dyed bob, turned up at their table like a middle-aged, and very determined, elf. She clapped her hands. "Listen up, Marty and all! There are taxis outside to take us to the karaoke. Marty, you need to settle the bill." She guided him away.

As they were leaving, Tim took Kat aside. "Amy thinks you aren't a karaoke fan," he said.

"No," she admitted.

"I've got a hotel room just the other side of St Paul's Square," he told her. "Two minutes' walk. Think you can manage it?"

She glanced around for Amy. Her friend was just stepping into a cab with Erik.

Tim's younger brother, Dan, dashed after Amy. "Room for one more in that cab?" He winked and waved at Tim.

Kat realised how much she'd had to drink. "I'll bale out with you," she told Tim, draping her leopard-print mac around her shoulders.

"Allow me," Tim said, removing it and helping her arms into the coat. "It's mild for December, but not that warm."

He held her close, supporting her as they walked uphill through St Paul's churchyard. The handsome white church loomed in front of them, and then to their right as they crossed the square.

Marty was smart: there were hotels springing up all around the centre of Birmingham. Their destination, a modern grey cuboid which looked out of place amongst its Victorian Gothic neighbours, lay in a side street not far from the converted jewellery workshop where Erik and Amy had flats. Kat supposed her brother and best friend were singing with the rest of Marty's workforce, most of them young people who had been born after Duran Duran's heyday.

Tim checked in, showing the receptionist an email on his phone.

Belatedly, Kat wondered why he'd splashed out. As if echoing her thoughts, he said, "Dad's paying. Tanya booked the hotel for him, in case he was too drunk to go home. But I've checked with Angela, and she's collecting him from the karaoke bar. It's a cheap room, and small, but it's got everything we need."

The bed, veiled in white, occupied half the space. Kat took off her coat and heels, lay down, and stretched. "Mmm, it's comfortable," she said. "Care to join me?"

Tim smiled. "Did I tell you earlier that your dress is fabulous?" he said. "Of course, I like what's in it even more."

Kat's little black number was expensive and skimpy, a relic of the time when she'd lived with Ross in London and had more money than love. She pulled Tim into an embrace, feeling him unzip the back of the garment and ease it off.

He kissed her, teasing the tip of her tongue with his. The dress was suddenly a puddle of fabric on the floor.

Tim breathed in sharply. "You're wearing stockings, Kat?"

"Just for you." She'd expected to take him home.

Tim fondled her breasts, slipping off her silky bra and then her knickers. He began to kiss her thighs.

Kat lounged on the bed, excitement rising, happy for once for Tim to take the lead. "Aren't you going to undress as well?" she asked.

"In due time," Tim said. He flicked his tongue to the point where her legs joined, teasing her, his fingers reaching to pinch her nipples. "I don't think you're ready," he said, his voice husky.

Kat felt herself flush. "I am," she protested, pulling his mouth towards hers. She fumbled with his shirt buttons.

"Perhaps you are," he said. Swiftly, he unbuckled his belt to show her that he was too. He threw his clothes onto the floor and entered her.

Kat relaxed, moving in time with her lover, basking in the excitement she saw in his eyes. Waves of intense pleasure filled her. Although usually controlled, she found herself screaming Tim's name as their passion reached its mutual peak.

Tim withdrew. He stroked her hair, tenderly placing a towel beneath her bottom. She hadn't noticed the fluffy white cloth before; perhaps it had been lying, folded, beside the bed.

"It's just as well you didn't go singing with the others," he murmured. "They'd have heard you in Coventry."

"Want a shower?" Kat asked. She was suddenly energised.

"Who knows? Maybe we'll start again afterwards," Tim said.

As he began running the shower in the adjacent wetroom, Kat reclined on the bed. She was going to enjoy every minute of this unexpected Christmas bonus.

71

Chapter 18.   Shaun

"Merry Christmas," the screw said, his tone bored as he unlocked Shaun's cell. "We're going to the chapel. Don't be late!"

Sidey shuffled after him as Shaun joined the cons being led to the circular space that served as a religious meeting-place for every denomination in the prison. It was a chance to stretch their legs, although the journey was slow because of the repeated unlocking and locking of metal gates that occurred on the way.

"You're looking thin, Al. Losing weight?" This was a lag who had just returned to the wing after a month of solitary confinement.

Shaun was tempted to tell him to go to the top of the class, but resisted. "A bit. Merry Christmas, by the way."

"You seen a doctor?"

"He gave me aspirin," Shaun said. It was the medic's standard remedy, but Shaun couldn't fault him this time. His shrinking waistline resulted from spurning the stodge with which Belmarsh bulked out the prisoners' meals. Tea-time sandwiches found their way to Sidey. Shaun ate little but protein, vegetables and fruit.

It was a balancing act. He was aiming to lose enough weight to secure a hospital referral, but without actually putting his health at risk. To be certain of holding his own in a fight, he still worked his muscles in the gym every day, although he wasn't taking black market steroids anymore.

The lag scowled. "Keep on at him, Al. Don't let him fob you off."

They filed into the chapel. Shaun quickly looked around for Jon and the other wing bosses.

This was nominally an Anglican service, with all the prayers and hymns that involved. Many prisoners stumbled through them. Spiritual guidance wasn't high on their agenda. They were here to gain respite from their cells, and to network. Any prisoner who could plausibly claim allegiance to the Church of England did so on admission to Belmarsh, regardless of their familiarity with the order of service.

Today, Shaun was looking forward to a longer ceremony in Jon's company, with plenty of loud carols to mask their conversation. The feast day fell on a Sunday this year, so the weekly price-fixing, score-settling and intelligence-swapping would take place as usual. While much of the business was conducted on illicit mobile phones, there was no substitute for seeing the whites of a man's eyes.

Shaun stood next to his son, waiting for one of the better-known carols to begin. 'Once in Royal David's City' was always popular. As the prisoners belted out the first verse, Shaun turned to Jon. "Merry Christmas, son," he whispered.

"Merry Christmas, Dad."

"It will be. We've got hooch."

"I can do better," Jon said. "Vince sent in good stuff. A little Christmas treat."

More rumours had reached Shaun's ears. He decided to have it out with Jon once and for all. "Really? You're telling me he's no more than a friend?" he said, trying to sound casual.

"Like I said before, we're just mates, Dad," Jon hissed.

"Nothing more than that?" Shaun asked, peering at his son's blue eyes. They were innocent as a baby's.

"No, Dad."

"I've heard otherwise. First, it was Lesley Mowatt..."

"That cow. It's none of her business." Jon paused. "It's no one's business. But I don't need people, anyhow. Not the way Vince does. Not like you do."

"Me? What do you mean?" Shaun snarled as he flushed. He surely couldn't let that go. He'd worked hard for his reputation, one that inspired fear and respect in equal measure.

"You needed Mum," Jon said. "I did too, once. Not now." He lowered his voice. "We'll get you out of here, Dad - out of it. Nothing else matters. Not who I have sex with, okay? That's just for convenience. It could be anyone, and it doesn't mean anything. But maybe I need Vince to believe it does. He'd have gone into meltdown if I hadn't talked him out of it."

"What's he got to complain about?" Shaun asked. "He's on the out."

He saw Jon's hands tense to fists, then relax. "Vince wouldn't say anything to you, and he'd look all right, but he isn't. I told him, don't get mad, get even. He said he already did that, but the pressure's getting to him."

His son was talking in riddles. "You say Vince is falling apart without you. I've got no chance of getting out then," Shaun said bitterly. "Ben's as much use as an ice-cream van in hell. Soft to the point of melting. I should never have let your mum send him to Sunday school. Lucky I'd learned my lesson by the time you were old enough."

73

"Don't talk about Mum like that," Jon said. His gaze hardened as if a switch had been flicked.

"Sorry." Shaun realised he'd lost the high ground. He noted Jon hadn't defended his brother.

Jon shrugged. "Vince will hold it together with my help," he promised. "He's had the odd bender, done too much coke, but he's staying off the skag and spice, unlike our customers in here. They're crazy."

"Tell me about it," Shaun said.

"You always said prison was a young man's game," Jon mused. "You can't hack it in the nick forever, Dad, so we have to get you out. Vince has a gun. As soon as you swing a transfer to hospital, he'll come for you."

"I'd take you with me if I could," Shaun said.

Jon shook his head. "I'll do my bird. All right, in time, I'll cut Vince loose and get another supplier. I've made contacts in here. It may be boring inside, but it's an easy way to make money, the easiest I know."

"Sales good on your wing, then?" Shaun asked. He was hardly satisfied with Jon's explanation, but it was clear his son would say nothing more.

"Yes, well up for Christmas," Jon replied.

The last strains of the carol ended. Shaun passed his son a coded price list. Jon nodded, giving it to another wing boss next to him. They had a more lively business chat during 'O Come All Ye Faithful', although the quiet verse in the middle nearly caught Jon out.

The service ended with 'Hark The Herald Angels Sing'. Shaun hugged his son. "Merry Christmas," he repeated, before filing out of the chapel for the slow walk back to his cell.

He ignored Sidey and the others, his head full of past Christmases with Meg. They had been family fun times in which religion didn't figure at all. The two boys would stagger out of bed mid-morning for their lavishly wrapped presents; latterly, the tell-tale square boxes of video games. There would be lunch: huge plates of turkey with all the trimmings served to at least a dozen family members. Shaun and the men would repair to the White Horse afterwards. The women and children stayed behind with a mountain of chocolates, Baileys and computer games.

At least two hundred cards festooned his lounge in Wanstead each year. In his cell, by contrast, he could count on his fingers the envelopes that awaited him today. Shaun had delayed opening them, planning to occupy himself before the pale parody of a festive meal that would be provided later. Now, he rolled a cigarette while he read the seasonal wishes of goodwill from devoted family and friends.

Shaun recognised all the handwriting apart from one envelope, postmarked London. He opened this first, puzzled to see a picture of a chubby Victorian gent framed by a holly wreath.

As soon as he read the message inside, he realised who had sent him, according to the card label, a portrait of Oscar Wilde: playwright and famous gay. Marshall Jenner, a disgraced MP, had once been Shaun's cellmate. They'd rubbed along amicably, despite the MP's predilection for younger men. Shaun didn't consider himself homophobic, but then, Marshall wasn't his beloved son.

'Dear Al', he read, 'You'll have heard that, after a brief "holiday" on the coast, my appeal against a custodial sentence was successful. I'll be spending Christmas with my wife, who is standing by me. Best wishes for the festive season, Jens.'

Knowing Jens still had time for him felt like the finest Christmas present ever. Thanks to his heiress wife, Jens had money and contacts. If anyone could ensure an ailing con received medical treatment, it was the former MP.

Shaun retrieved his notepad. 'It's great to hear from you, Jens,' he wrote. 'Merry Christmas! I'm rather down in the dumps, in spite of the turkey leg and Christmas pud. I'm sure I've got prostate cancer…'

Chapter 19.   Kat

"And here it is," Erik announced proudly, "a Bazaki beef stew with dumplings." He towered over his sister. Tall and thin, he nearly bumped into the ceiling of his attic flat as he placed the dish on a table laid for two.

"The best Christmas dinner ever," Kat said. "As long as we start with a toast of vodka."

She'd brought a bottle from her latest batch. Taking it out of her bag, she nipped into Erik's galley kitchen for a couple of shot glasses. Having stayed in his tiny flat before, she knew where to look.

"Your good health," she said, filling the shot glasses.

"And yours," Erik said, knocking one of them back.

It was traditional in Bazakistan to toast your parents. Kat glanced at Erik's graduation photograph. A schoolgirl version of herself, sandwiched between Erik and her father, beamed back. Their mother, a hand on Erik's arm, smiled too. The woman who now answered to Marina Aliyeva was coolly blonde, her husband dark-haired, green-eyed and handsome like their son.

Erik followed her gaze. A shadow passed across his face. "No. We're English now," he said. "Cheers."

Kat sipped her drink. Perhaps it was the thought of her father, betrayed by his wife to the state for political reasons, that made the vodka unappealing. "This doesn't taste right," she said.

Erik wrapped his arms around her. "Kat, there's nothing wrong with it. You make the best vodka on the planet."

"That's an intriguing strapline for Starshine," she said. "I'll run it past Amy."

"Let's sit down and eat," Erik said. "Afterwards, we'll have that British speciality, the Christmas pudding. I bought one at the supermarket."

He spooned large portions of stew onto their plates, far more than she'd usually eat. "It's Christmas," he said, grinning.

"Happy days," Kat said. "This is delicious." If it hadn't been, she'd have lied. She was grateful for the invitation.

"I learned how to cook as a student," Erik said. "It was how I coped on a budget. I've long suspected that your solution was different. You just didn't eat."

"Could be," Kat admitted. She didn't see any problem with a diet of coffee and cigarettes, although she could microwave a meal and chill wine as well as anyone else.

"I wish Amy was here," Erik said suddenly. "It would be wonderful to spend Christmas Day with both the women I love. She's with Charles today, and seeing her mother tomorrow."

"That's kind of normal," Kat said. "If you were married, you'd have to go with her."

"Married?" Erik looked shocked. "What's she been saying to you?"

"Relax," Kat said. "Amy hasn't dropped the slightest hint that she expects a ring on her finger. She's also unimpressed by the trouble and expense that Dee and Charles are going to. If nothing else, that would put her off. Dee's dress alone is costing twenty thousand pounds."

"Dee's a millionaire, so she'd expect nothing less."

"Hasn't Amy said anything to you about it at all, Erik? Here she is, in a tiny flat in Birmingham, and they're spending all this money on themselves. If you add up the designer dresses, top musicians and high-end hotel, they could have bought her a property instead."

"I guess Charles would, if the money were his," Erik said. "Most parents want to help their children out."

Kat's lips tightened. "Except our mother. And Marty Bridges. Tim's had to pay for his flat himself."

"Marty gave him a job," Erik said.

"On condition he didn't go to university," Kat pointed out. "And he's not paying Tim well. Or either of us, for that matter." Her resentment was in full flow. "I wasn't even invited to Christmas lunch with Marty, along with Tim and his siblings."

"You're not married," Erik said.

Kat laughed. "That was quick, Erik. You're right. And I'd rather spend Christmas with you." She felt a pang of longing for Tim, though. She'd phoned him already before setting off to see her brother, but now she resolved to call again.

She seized her chance when Erik was occupied in the kitchen, heating the pudding.

Tim answered speedily. "I'm missing you too," he said, his words coinciding with the microwave's ping. "Are you wearing your present? Pretty in pink?"

"Yes. Want to see it?" She had unwrapped the delicate wisps of flowery lace and silk that morning. Tim had chosen the pastel colours she loved. He was so thoughtful. Ross, her ex, would have ignored her preferences and chosen black or red.

"How about Boxing Day brunch?" Tim asked. "Are you staying at your brother's to sleep off the hangover?"

"Yes, I'll be couch-surfing here, but…"

Tim cut in. "Hang on, Kat. Angela wants a word."

Not Marty himself, but his second wife, Kat thought bitterly. "Hello?" she said.

"Merry Christmas," Angela trilled. At least she sounded sincere.

"Merry Christmas," Kat replied, trying to inject enthusiasm into her voice.

"We're having a New Year's Eve get-together," Angela said. "I'd love you to join us. Are you free?"

"I'll check my diary," Kat lied.

"Erik and Amy are welcome, too." Angela said.

Erik emerged from the kitchen with a full tray. "Ready to light the brandy?" he asked. "Oh, you're on the phone."

"Angela's asked us round on New Year's Eve."

A smile lit his face. "Great."

Kat surrendered to the inevitable. "Count us in."

Socialising with Marty wasn't high on her wish list. She'd just have to spend the evening avoiding him.

Chapter 20.   Vince

Dusk was falling when Vince's phone rang. He recognised the number immediately. "Merry Christmas, Jon," he said. "How's it going?"

"Party time," Jon said. "I've had hooch, whizz and weed. The screws won't bust us over Christmas; it's too much aggro."

Vince almost wished he was there. He gazed towards the window of his mother's low-rise council flat, which was surrounded by similar apartment blocks. West Ham was quieter than the Tottenham High Road, but hardly lovelier. He appreciated the flashing fairy lights and five-foot-high glowing snowman on Lesley Mowatt's balcony. They improved the view.

"You're at your mum's, I suppose," Jon said. "Can I talk to her?"

It was a command rather than a request. "She's sozzled on sherry already," Vince said.

Jon cursed. "Give her a message when she's sober then, will you? She's still shooting her mouth off and she's to shut it. It's bad for her health if she doesn't. Understand? My dad's not happy."

Vince felt dizzy, as if a chasm had opened at his feet. He wobbled on the brink. "I told her to be careful, but when she's had a drink…"

"That's her problem," Jon said. "It's up to her to fix it, if she knows what's good for her. My dad's been hearing gossip. Lucky he doesn't believe it." His voice softened. "You know how it is, Vince. He'd kill us both. It's our secret, right?"

"Right," Vince said. "We'll still be together, though, won't we? When you come out?"

"Of course. It'll be just like before."

Vince was infused with a sense of relief. Despite the risks, Jon cared. A future sharing his divided affections, however furtive, was infinitely better than life without him.

He glanced at his mother, almost unconscious on her threadbare sofa, her greying hair dishevelled. Tension coursed through him again. "Got to go. Love you."

"You too, mate." Obviously, Jon had to choose his words carefully. He was in a cell with a straight guy. Belmarsh was the kind of place where you were never alone.

"Who was that?" Lesley Mowatt's speech was slurred.

"Never mind, Mum. Go back to sleep."

"You're a good boy, Vince," she said, woozily.

There was no point communicating Shaun's threats until she'd dried out. The task must wait for another day. Vince tidied up around her, taking the remnants of their lunch into the kitchen. He put the remains of the turkey crown in a bowl with a clean dinner plate on top, and placed it in the fridge. It was just as well he'd learned cookery at school, as his mother had lost interest in it since his father's death. Her decline had been steady from that point.

When Meg Halloran had died, Vince had hoped Shaun would take a romantic interest in Lesley. Both were without a partner and of a similar age. Vince saw how naïve he'd been, not just in thinking an alcoholic widow would attract a man who didn't share her addiction, but in letting himself be dazzled by Shaun's wealth and power. Now he was caught in the Hallorans' web, dependent on them for love and money.

Should he help Shaun escape, knowing the man had threatened his mother's life, and by extension, his own? He had no choice: it was what Jon wanted, and Jon couldn't be denied.

She began to snore. He washed the dishes and cleaned the kitchen. It didn't take long. It wasn't as if his mother aped Ben Halloran in her approach to housework; she still adhered to basic standards. He envied her, floating in a boozy dream, oblivious to the still-blaring television and the cares that gripped her son's soul. Tiptoeing, he left the flat, locking the door behind him.

Outside, the street was deserted, cloaked in the boredom that had characterised most of Vince's childhood. Brightly lit windows and occasional sounds of revelry were the only clues that others lived in this rectangular grid of homes. The weather was mild for the season, cloud obscuring the moon and stars. Bookies who had taken bets on a white Christmas would be laughing all the way to the bank.

Vince delved into a pocket for his phone, intending to take his chances on finding a cab back to Tottenham. Instead, he speed-dialled another number.

It was a mistake. His finger slipped. He realised as soon as the phone began ringing and a name appeared on its screen. It was someone he'd met online, over a year before.

Vince hadn't fancied him then, and he didn't now. The sex was tolerable, however, because this acquaintance was fun, and he had money. Wasn't he Shaun's friend too? Perhaps he'd be useful.

The phone was answered.

"Marshall?" Vince said. "I've got more Charlie than you'd believe. Want to help me get through it?"

Chapter 21.   Kat

"Gin and tonic?" Angela asked. "Or will that be vodka, Kat?" Marty's wife, sparkling in a blue sequinned dress and matching six-inch heels, stood beside a well-stocked drinks cabinet. Her blonde curls were adorned with a glittering alice band, her face made up with an expert hand.

"Just tonic," Kat told her beaming hostess. "I've got a tummy bug." While she hadn't been sick, the thought of alcohol nauseated her.

Angela handed her a large, bowl-shaped glass. Lemon slices and ice floated in the fizzy liquid. "Here you are, bab. Schweppes slimline." She winked. "I won't have the sugary stuff in the house."

Marty's white stuccoed mansion, occupying a tree-lined plot in the wealthier end of Edgbaston, was impressively large. Kat had visited it as a child, and recalled how rambling it had seemed, strewn with toys and sports gear by Tim and his siblings. Now the younger generation had moved out, the property had the air of a show home. Angela had installed cream carpets, pastel paint and tasteful artwork.

The doorbell rang. Tim brought Erik and Amy through to the front room. They were both smarter, glossier versions of their usual selves: Erik had donned a suit, and Amy a black velvet tunic. She was even wearing lipstick.

Erik kissed Angela's cheek. "You look fabulous."

Angela simpered. "Thank you. I hit the sales early. I've bought my outfit for the wedding of the century already."

"You mean Charles and Dee's?" Erik asked. "It isn't until March."

"I've found the perfect dress," Angela said. "Want to see it later? Amy, you can tell me if Dee would approve."

"Marty mentioned you were a fan," Erik said.

"Yes," Angela said. "Doesn't Dee look young for her age? I'd love to know how she does it. Is it the yoga? I do ten minutes with one of her DVDs every morning. Great for reducing stress."

"I prefer gin," Tim said. "Any chance of another splash, Angela?"

"Of course." She obliged. "Erik and Amy, what would you like to drink? G&T?"

Tim shepherded Kat into the drawing room. "You know most of my family, don't you?"

Dan, his sister Martha, and many of Tim's cousins were part of Marty's team at East West Bridges. Kat's recollection of the others was dim. At least a dozen of the clan gathered around her, asking how she'd enjoyed the holiday, and introducing her to uncles, aunts and friends.

Kat tried to ignore the sensation of being on display. She glimpsed Marty, sitting with other guests in a conservatory at the opposite end of the room.

"Top-up?" Angela asked, sloshing gin into Kat's glass before she could protest. "I don't suppose Tim's taken you over to his grandparents yet." She waved a red gel-tipped index finger, signalling to Kat to follow as she teetered towards the conservatory in her improbable heels. "They'll be pleased to see us. Marty's mum does enjoy her gin."

Checking no one was looking her way, Kat tipped her drink into the pot of a handily placed peace lily. She let Angela guide her to a cluster of lush plants and cushioned wicker furniture. Here, Marty was holding court to an elderly couple.

"This is Kat," Angela announced, stopping Marty mid-sentence.

The old man rose slowly to his feet. His joints were obviously painful. He couldn't straighten his back, but he inched towards Kat and held out a hand in greeting. "So, this is Tim's young lady. I'm Derek Bridges, and this is my wife, Sylvia."

Sylvia smiled at Kat. "I remember when you were a little girl. It's nice to see you again, dear. When Angela mentioned Tim's girlfriend was called Kat, I didn't twig it was you."

"My goodness, my lady wife's right," Derek said. "I do apologise. There were so many children running in and out of this house when our grandkids were small, I couldn't keep track of them all."

Kat had only the haziest memories of the pair herself. "You're looking well," she managed.

"You must forgive me, dear," Sylvia said. "I'll have to stay seated."

Kat noticed the woman's thin, frail appearance, and the walking stick resting on her chair. Having borne a bony handshake from Derek, she bent down to kiss Sylvia's cheek.

Derek chuckled. "I hope you haven't marked her with your lipstick, bab."

"Oh, don't worry," Sylvia said, clasping Kat's right hand in both of hers. They were beautifully manicured in the French style, rather than the gel nails favoured by Angela. "Thanks for coming over to say hello, dear. We've heard so much about you, haven't we, Derek?"

"All good, of course," Angela said.

"It's about time Tim settled down," Sylvia said. "We're not getting any younger. I want a great-grandchild before I pop my clogs."

Taken aback, Kat glanced at Marty. His face reflected a storm about to break.

"Aren't you being a bit hasty, Sylv?" Derek asked. "They've not been seeing each other long." He chortled, sounding spookily like Marty. "Don't let her wish your life away for you, bab."

Tim belatedly joined them. "Have you got the gin, Angela?"

"Do excuse my manners," Angela said, pouring generous measures into everyone's glasses. "Oops, the bottle's empty. I'll get some more, and champagne to ring in the New Year. Will you help me, please, Kat?"

Kat took the lifeline. "No problem," she said. "See you later."

"Don't mind the old folks," Angela said, once she'd steered Kat into the kitchen, out of the clan's earshot. "They're in your face, but there's no harm in them." She lowered her voice to a whisper. "How come you're not drinking? Don't pretend you are. I clocked the peace lily taking a soaking. Marty told me you were a party girl. I even bought in extra."

It wasn't just the elders who asked personal questions, then. "I'm not feeling well," Kat said. She still wasn't sure how she'd cope with her return to work on Tuesday. The production process relied on her tasting skills. She hoped she'd recover in time.

Angela persisted. "Are you pregnant?" she asked.

Kat shook her head. She hadn't even considered the possibility. In truth, she didn't know. To her growing dismay, memories of the Christmas party began to crystallise. There had been a night in a hotel with Tim. Had she nipped back home for a pill in the morning? When she recalled the hangover she'd suffered, she doubted it. Would pregnancy affect her that quickly, though? It wasn't even two weeks ago.

A baby wasn't part of her plan. She needed to make a success of her business, prove herself to Marty, and reap the rewards. He was paying her a basic salary, but she'd have a share when Starshine vodka made profits. She knew the brand would be a money-spinner: as soon as she moved to larger premises, she could show Marty that. Her future lay in her own hands, and a child was a wild card.

84

How would Tim feel? Kat had dreamed about walking down the aisle with him, but he hadn't asked. Whatever Sylvia thought, they'd never talked about a long-term future, or children.

She hadn't experienced any maternal instincts either. Didn't they suddenly appear when you hit thirty? This was way too soon. Kat shuddered.

Angela sensed Kat's uncertainty. "I bet we can find out," Marty's wife said conspiratorially. "Tim's cousin, Lucy, is bound to have a pregnancy test in her handbag. She's trying for a baby, you know."

"That's kind of you, but no thanks," Kat said, her head beginning to spin. She suspected a test wouldn't work this early. Anyway, the last thing she needed was confirmation of her worst fears in front of Marty, Tim and two dozen of their kinfolk.

Marty marched into the kitchen. He scowled at Kat. "I thought you were fetching gin," he complained to Angela.

"Yes, boss. I'm on it like a car bonnet," she said, giving a mock salute and handing him a bottle of Langley's No 8.

Marty read the label. "London Dry Gin?"

"It's made in the Black Country."

"That's better," he conceded. "I remember Dom Davis pimping it in his club now. What were you two discussing, anyway?"

"Just girl talk," Angela replied.

Chapter 22.   Vince

"We'll have champagne." Marshall Jenner, former MP and jailbird, turned to Vince. "Do you have a preference?"

"Craft beer," Vince said.

Marshall chuckled. His double chin wobbled. Coupled with his bald dome, the effect was of Humpty Dumpty falling off the wall. "You hipsters! You can't decline champagne at the Ritz. It's against the rules." He nodded to the waiter, a smooth young man with a professional smile. "Make that a bottle of house champagne. And we'll have an extra glass with a Guinness, please."

As the lad returned to the bar, Marshall said, "If you must have beer, take it in a Black Velvet."

"Twist my arm, then," Vince said, relaxing into his pony-skin chair. "I like this place already." He didn't rate the rough boozers that Shaun favoured; Shoreditch's upmarket haunts were more his style, but the Rivoli Bar's polished wood and plush seats outclassed them all for opulence and kitsch. Vince had the sense that, here, no irony was intended.

Marshall's clothes cut a dash, as if he were campaigning for re-election. He wore a tailored suit that gave no hint of the flabby figure beneath. The pale shirt and silk tie flattered his blue eyes rather than his florid skin. "I'm glad you're properly dressed," he remarked.

"A dicky bow, you mean?" As usual, Vince sported a white shirt, red braces, black waistcoat and smart trousers. He'd added a bow tie in honour of the venue.

"They don't like trainers," Marshall said. "Not a problem for you." He pointed to Vince's feet, clad in gleaming black winklepickers. "Once, they tried to stop Jeannie from entering. In the end, she walked in barefoot."

"What happened?" Vince asked, bristling at the mention of Marshall's wife but curious nonetheless.

"We enjoyed a glass of champagne together," Marshall said. "Jeannie usually gets her own way."

"Really?" Vince asked. "She's happy about our little reunion, then?"

Marshall patted his hand. "What she doesn't know, won't hurt her."

"How much is that peace of mind worth?" Vince asked.

Marshall took it as a joke. "Cheeky boy. Jeannie's never cared about my little bit of fun, so long as I don't flaunt it in front of her. She took me back after I'd been in prison, remember." He sighed. "It was a wake-up call for her. After the media storm about rent boys, she realised she'd let herself go. She needed to raise her game. While I was inside, she lost three stone and had her nose fixed. Look." He took the latest iPhone from his pocket, showing Vince a photograph of an elegant blonde of middle years. "What do you think?"

"All right," Vince said. "She looks better than my mum." He guessed the two women must be about the same age. Marshall himself, bald and wrinkled, was well on the way to collecting a pension. "I can't really comment. I don't do women."

"Alas, nor do I," Marshall confided. "It's a shame, after all the trouble she's been to, and the expense. The hairdresser, plastic surgeon and personal trainer don't come cheap."

"Maybe I'm in the wrong job," Vince said.

Marshall leaned forward. "What is your job?" he asked. "I don't think it's ever cropped up in conversation."

Vince was saved from answering by the champagne's arrival.

"I'm sorry, Sir, we have no Guinness," the waiter said. "I do have stout from an independent brewery, though."

"Craft beer? Bring it on," Vince said.

The bottles were opened for them. "A Black Velvet in this glass, Sir?" the waiter asked. He poured a little stout into the flute, topping it up with foamy champagne before placing it in front of Vince.

"Santé," Marshall said, picking up the other glass. "Sorry I couldn't see you on Christmas Day. I was cruising in the Caribbean. Before you ask, it wasn't that kind of cruising, more's the pity."

Vince tried the jet-coloured cocktail, expecting an abomination. It wasn't at all bad. He was reminded of the gassy ciders he'd sampled as a teenager.

"I've paid cash for the room," Marshall said. "Otherwise, it would go on my credit card, and Jeannie would see it. She's tolerant, but there's no need to force it down her throat. We can't go back to your flat, can we, because you live with someone?"

"He moved out," Vince said, without mentioning Jon was detained at Her Majesty's pleasure. "But my place is in Tottenham, anyway. Do you know it? You wouldn't want to go there." Marshall wasn't used to that sort of area, nor it to him. Vince imagined the ex-MP strolling down the High Road with his Savile Row suit, Rolex and air of entitlement. It wouldn't end well.

"Oh yes. I crossed swords with your MP back in the day," Marshall said. "A principled man, but the other side of the political divide. I can't say I miss the House of Commons anymore. My little legal problem with expense claims taught me who my friends were. I've heard from a handful of members since I left the house, but I've had far more approaches from the prisoners I met in Belmarsh."

"Let me guess," Vince said. "They're down on their luck, and they want money."

"A few of them asked, yes," Marshall admitted. "I gave them tobacco, or burn, as they call it. They appreciated it. But mostly, people contact me about bigger problems. I was rather the agony aunt when I was inside. I shared a pad, as he might put it, with your chum, Shaun."

"I know," Vince said. He recalled the occasion when he'd visited Shaun, only to see Marshall across a crowded room. Jeannie had been sitting with her husband. She had been weightier, and her hair greyer, than the recent image. Vince's cheery wave had provoked a glare from her. He wondered if she were really as comfortable with her husband's sexuality as Marshall thought.

"It's terribly sad," Marshall said. "Shaun tells me he has prostate cancer."

"Yes, he's in a bad way," Vince said, hopeful that Marshall could be enlisted in Shaun's escape plan. "He'll be dead in two months without proper treatment, and he isn't getting it."

"I suppose the doctors only give him aspirin," Marshall said. "That was all they did for me when I caught flu. I found them most unsympathetic."

"Exactly," Vince said gloomily. "It's so unfair." He widened his eyes, attempting a puppyish expression. "You have friends in high places, Marshall. Can't you get him out on compassionate grounds?"

Marshall began to melt. "I can't promise that, but I'm sure I can pull strings to secure medical treatment for him."

This was working like a charm. "Shaun should be in hospital," Vince said. "He needs specialist care, not analgesics."

Marshall looked at him sharply. "That's a big word for you."

"I've got GCSEs," Vince said. "Just because I live in Tottenham, it doesn't mean I'm thick. I hang out in Hoxton most of all, anyway."

"Isn't that rough too?" Marshall asked.

Vince stifled a snigger. "You're more likely to get a latte than get mugged in Hoxton Square," he said. "Is there any champagne left? Otherwise, I'm swigging the rest of that stout out of the bottle."

Marshall attacked the ice bucket. "No," he reported. "Let's go upstairs. Do you have any, you know, Charlie with you?"

"Sweet white dreams coming up," Vince said. "Can you reimburse me? That stuff's expensive." Everyone else paid him for cocaine. He didn't see why Marshall should be different.

Marshall fidgeted. "I don't buy drugs."

"Think of it as boosting my finances," Vince said. "A late Christmas present."

Marshall appeared to relax. This was obviously familiar ground for him. "Of course. I'll always help a young friend out. Let's have more champagne sent up to the room. Ready?"

Chapter 23.   Kat

Kat's alarm sounded at six. Bleary-eyed, she staggered out of bed. Sleep had been fitful at best. Now, awake once more, she struggled with the question that had occupied her mind during the night: was she expecting Tim's child?

After the grilling by Angela, she'd googled pregnancy tests. Apparently, they weren't reliable until two weeks after conception. She was over that hurdle this morning, her first day back at work.

Her usual routine involved a bus, sometimes two, but always a stroll through the city centre. Marty had snapped up old factories and warehouses on its fringes, planning to turn a profit as Birmingham's core expanded. One of the run-down properties housed the Starshine distillery. Kat's route took her past several pharmacies, all of them open early to catch morning commuter trade.

She hovered at the door of the first of these before marching inside. Rows of brightly coloured cosmetics, skin and hair products bombarded her vision. Where were the test kits? She headed for the medicine counter at the rear of the store.

There was an array of boxes on display, all promising fast, reliable results. Kat had no idea which to choose.

"I always use this one." A heavily pregnant young shop assistant, perky in her smart uniform, pointed to a lurid pink and blue box.

"Thanks."

"You're welcome." The girl beamed at her. "It's your first, isn't it? I can tell. How exciting!"

Kat plastered a smile on her face, freezing it there until she'd paid at the till.

Even though the box was light, it seemed to weigh down her handbag like a lump of lead. Her steps slowed. She realised she was staring at a shop window crammed with babywear. Kat's stomach heaved.

She was rarely this jumpy. Although she'd given up smoking, she stopped at a newsagent for a pack of Silk Cut and a lighter. Fingers trembling, she lit a cigarette.

She had no chance to experience the tranquillising effect of nicotine. The smell triggered a fresh surge of nausea. Kat threw the packet away.

While she managed a small team now, none of them were there yet. Kat was always first in and last out, unlocking and locking up her ground floor premises. She didn't encounter other occupants of the three-storey redbrick building, either. After Marty had reconfigured it for the distillery, some space remained on the upper floors. He'd rented it to a T-shirt printer and a man who stored Christmas decorations there. Neither had expected the first week of January to be busy, and she wasn't surprised to hear no footsteps above her.

In the shared ground floor washroom, she opened the testing kit and read the instructions carefully. She was to place the tip of the plastic detector in a flow of urine, wait a few seconds, then check the result.

It was bound to be negative, wasn't it? How silly to panic. Kat looked at her watch, feeling blood pulse through her temples as time moved slower than she'd thought possible. She counted: one, two, three, four.

The test was positive.

Kat re-read the instructions. She'd done everything right. There was a blue line, and a cross. It couldn't be wrong.

She suddenly felt both alone and too crowded, her body invaded by an unwelcome stranger.

Despite sleepless nights and imagined conversations, she still couldn't guess how Tim would react. Was their relationship strong enough for this? She was sure it would never survive if she simply terminated the pregnancy without a word. Either the secret would gnaw at her soul, or it would spill out and split them apart. However tempting it was to let ambition lead her down that path, she had to tell him.

Kat picked up the phone, hoping as she hit speed-dial that the call would go to voicemail.

"Kat." Tim's voice boomed cheerily from his hands-free set, as if he was already two coffees to the good. "What's new? I'm driving - just about to join the M6 toll road."

"I'm sorry, Tim. I'm pregnant."

There was a pause. Kat closed her eyes, wishing she'd found a better way to express herself.

"Whew. I didn't expect that," Tim said. He sounded anxious. "Are you at work? I'll be straight round."

The clock ticked slowly. She'd mapped out the morning's tasks in her mind, but found herself pacing the distillery floor, devoid of focus. Finally, she stood on the pavement outside, watching traffic go by until his gold Subaru slid to a halt in front of her.

"Tim?"

He glanced at his watch as he stepped from the car. "Under thirty minutes," he said. "Good going." Grinning like a clown, he enveloped her in a bear hug. "This is marvellous news. How are you?"

"Shocked," Kat said. She may as well be honest. "I'm so close to achieving my dream. Your dad's showing faith in me at last. He's planning a significant investment in Starshine. Now I'm pregnant. I don't know how to make this work."

Tim kissed her lips. "We'll make it work together."

For a second, cocooned in his arms, she could believe it. Then Marty intruded on her thoughts again. "What will your dad say?"

"I'm sure he'll be pleased too. We should tell him at once."

"I can't face it. Don't women wait until three months before informing their employers?" She didn't share Tim's confidence in Marty's attitude.

Tim stroked her hair. "It's not a normal employer-employee situation, is it? You're his business partner, and you can't afford to give him cause to mistrust you. Dad needs to know. That's why I've asked Tanya to book a meeting with him today."

She pulled away from him, dismayed that he hadn't asked her first. "Does he know what the meeting's about?"

"No, I didn't tell Tanya. I wanted Dad to hear it from us." Tim smiled. "We'll see him this afternoon. I can't wait."

It was obvious he wanted to keep the baby. Hard as it was to tell him the truth, she had to do it now, before he broadcast the news. "I'm not the motherly sort," Kat said. "I'm considering a termination."

Tim's eager expression vanished. He stepped closer and wrapped his arms around her again. "Don't," he said. "Please?"

His blue eyes, wide with concern, held hers. "You really shouldn't worry," he said. "You'll love the baby when it's born. Believe me."

Kat didn't. She was overcome by fear of the future. She'd either lose Tim or have an unwanted child. Neither option appealed.

Tim would be devastated if she didn't continue the pregnancy, though. For his sake alone, she had to do it. "All right," she whispered.

Chapter 24.   Marty

"Tanya, my angel," Marty said, "can you pop out for chocolate biscuits, please?" One of the perks of the area's de-industrialisation was the opening of three convenience stores within a five-minute radius.

"I thought you'd be on a diet again," Tanya said.

"My wife thinks I am," Marty said. "We know better." Alarmed by his expanding waist, as she seemed to be every January, Angela had announced that his New Year's resolution was to cut his carbs. While she held sway at home, he didn't see why he should take any notice in Florence Street.

"Well, I've brought some Quality Street in for the girls," Tanya said. "You can have a few of those with your morning coffee, and I'll buy biscuits later. By the way, Tim and Kat wanted to meet you. I put them in your calendar for four o'clock."

"Fine," Marty said. He settled down to work, thinking no more about the meeting until Tanya phoned to say his visitors were on the way.

He was about to ask her to fetch tea and biscuits, but thought better of it. It would only take one unguarded remark from Tim to Angela, and his wife would learn of his disobedience. "You'll be bringing in drinks, won't you?" he said to Tanya. "No need for nibbles too."

A white china teapot and cups were waiting in his office when his PA ushered Tim and Kat inside it.

"Sit down," Marty said. He remained in the imposing leather swivel chair behind his desk.

The room was large enough to accommodate a meeting table and half a dozen chairs. Tim pulled two of these closer to the desk, facing his father. He gestured to Kat to sit in one, taking the other for himself.

Despite his salesman's polish, Tim's body language was tense. His shoulders were crunched up near his ears. He leaned forward onto Marty's desk rather than lounging back. Kat, too, in a sombre black trouser suit, looked apprehensive.

"Who's dead?" Marty asked.

That elicited a grin from Tim. He almost relaxed. "I've got good news and bad news, Dad."

"I'll take the good news," Marty said.

"Well," Tim beamed at Kat, "it's all of a piece. We're pregnant." His nerves seemed to have vanished. Pride shone from his face.

Marty managed to hide his shock with a passable smile. "Congratulations," he said.

"Of course, we want to minimise the impact on the business," Kat said. Her poise was perfect and her voice calm, the accent that of an English aristocrat.

She owed a lot to her posh boarding school, Marty thought. "I assume there will be an effect on your personal lives as well," he said.

Kat had the grace to blush.

"We'll take it day by day," Tim said, reaching for her hand and squeezing it. "There's almost nine months to go, so we've got plenty of time to get ready."

"And that means we can ensure vodka production isn't interrupted," Kat said. "My team will step up, and I'll find temporary operatives and train them. The Starshine business plan won't suffer. Then I'll be back as soon as I get childcare sorted out."

Kat's green eyes gazed at Marty with apparent sincerity. He suspected she was trying to gauge his reactions. She'd see nothing to disappoint her; he'd make sure of that. "I'm delighted to hear of your dedication," he said. "Can you give me your proposals on timings and cost by, say, this time next week? Meanwhile, I'm afraid I have to go soon, as I have a commitment this evening."

For the first time in the meeting, Marty rose to his feet, knowing it would compel the young couple to do the same. As if acting a part, he clapped a hand on Tim's shoulder. "Congratulations, son," he repeated. Then, kissing Kat's cheek, he said, "Congratulations, bab."

Once they'd left, he sat at the desk again, his head in his hands. How could his son be so careless?

He should have realised Kat would never be satisfied with a half-share in Starshine vodka. She wanted all of Marty's business. It would be Tim's when Marty retired, giving Kat the opportunity to take what she pleased before discarding his son. There were financial difficulties right now, but he'd overcome them. It made him sick to think he was working so hard for Kat's benefit.

Marty tried to drink the rest of his tea. It tasted tepid and bitter. Finally, he packed his briefcase, donned his black wool winter coat and strode out of the room to his secretary's workstation.

"Tanya, I'm going to call it a day," he said. Eyes alighting on the packet of chocolate digestives, he added, "And I'll have a biccie or three for the road, please." He'd enjoy whatever small comforts life could still offer him.

His silver F-type Jag was another indulgence. There was no way he'd take it to the ton on his mile-long journey in the Birmingham rush hour, but he enjoyed a brief thrill at the Bristol Road traffic lights, accelerating from zero to forty miles per hour in what felt like a split second. It barely took the edge off his anger.

He unlocked his front door, removing his coat as the centrally heated air warmed his cheeks. A delicious smell permeated the spacious hallway. It was a shame that, whatever Angela was cooking, there wouldn't be enough of it.

His wife emerged from the kitchen, dusting off her hands. Apart from a few specks of flour, her grooming was immaculate. She was wearing a pale pink silk blouse, skinny jeans and fluffy mules with a three-inch heel. Marty, although of average height at best, still towered over her. A wave of relief washed over him. Unlike the sly and manipulative Kat, there was no side to Angela. She loved him, and just wanted to please. Even the diets she foisted on him were an attempt to serve his best interests.

"You're home early," she said.

"I'm just dropping the car off," he said. "I thought I'd go down the Harborne Club for a jar." He had no appointments that evening at all; the club was a place where he could expect decent beer, like-minded company and a sympathetic ear. With luck, he could have a convivial curry afterwards with a some of his buddies.

Angela looked puzzled. "It's not five thirty yet. The club won't be open."

"It will be by the time I've walked there." The route, downhill and sober, took around thirty minutes. He'd call a cab to come back later.

Her quizzical expression hadn't disappeared. "What's the matter, Marty?"

"It's like this," Marty said, determination cutting through the gloom in his voice. "Kat's pregnant, and I need a drink."

"I thought she was!" Angela said triumphantly. "That's wonderful. Let's crack open the champagne."

"You knew?" Marty asked, discomfited.

95

Angela tapped the side of her nose. "Call it a woman's intuition. Make yourself comfortable in the drawing room, and I'll bring the drinks through."

"If it's all the same to you," Marty said, "I'd rather have Two Towers Birmingham Mild. Lots of it."

"Each to their own," Angela said. "We've got a few bottles of that in the kitchen, as it happens. I'll fetch as many as you want."

Marty forbore from saying she couldn't. His desire for beer was enough to drink a brewery dry. He kicked off his shoes and slumped into the embrace of a plump vanilla-hued armchair.

"Here we are," Angela said brightly, placing a tray on the spotless coffee table. "I've just opened a quarter-bottle of champers for myself. I can always get another. Here's your beer." She poured mild into a glass and handed it to him, before helping herself to fizz.

"I don't know what you're so happy about," Marty said. "We don't even know if it's Tim's. Although he thinks it is."

Angela showed as much surprise as Botox allowed. "There's no need for that, Marty Bridges. Kat isn't a slapper."

"What makes you so sure?"

Angela tutted. "I've known Kat since she was small. Don't forget, I was your secretary in the days when you did business with her father. She was a nice little girl then, so why would you think she'd sleep around now?"

Marty shook his head, swigging his beer silently.

"It'll be lovely to have grandchildren around the place," Angela said wistfully.

"Really?" Marty pointed to the dove-grey walls and cream carpet. It was the antithesis of a child-friendly environment. "You've never had little ones running riot with jammy fingers."

He realised as he said it that he'd been tactless. At sixteen, Angela had given an illegitimate baby up for adoption. He reached over and patted her hand. "I know you'd have liked a family," he said, kindly. "We just weren't spring chickens anymore when we got together, bab."

"No use crying over spilt milk," Angela said, misty-eyed. She topped up her champagne flute with the rest of the tiny bottle.

"I'll get you another of those," Marty said, taking the opportunity to find more beer while he did so. He also checked the top shelves of the kitchen cupboards for chocolates, knowing this was where she hid sweets to deter herself from reaching for them too often. "Here you are, bab. A few brandy truffles won't spoil your appetite."

"Thanks." Angela popped one in her mouth. "You finish them, Marty. You can ease up on the diet occasionally; you've been sticking to it so well."

Marty did as he was told. He still couldn't chill, despite another bottle of mild. "I wish I'd never funded Kat's Starshine vodka," he said.

"Why?" Angela asked. "She can get cover when she's on maternity leave, can't she? I mean, she'll be back at work after a few months, I suppose. This is the twenty-first century, Marty."

"It's a story as old as time," Marty said. "Kat's taken advantage of Tim. She's trapped him."

Worse, she'd taken advantage of Marty too. He'd spent years building his business and defending it. Marina wasn't the first to attempt to rob him of the Snow Mountain brand through the law courts. Kat had already tried, and it was only when she failed that she'd developed Starshine.

That had been her foot in the door. Now he was dependent on her for Snow Mountain. If it hadn't been for Tim's involvement, Marty wouldn't have risked dealing with Kat, regardless of her distilling skills. Why hadn't he warned his son away from her?

Instead, Marty had begun to trust Kat enough to talk of his business plans at the Christmas party. That must have been the signal for her to strike. She'd steal his business through his weakest link: his son. Marty shuddered.

"Oh dear. Out of beer?" Angela asked.

"Yes." He didn't care if it was true or not. It was a convenient excuse to take his dark thoughts away from the bright light that Angela persisted in shining on them. "I'm going to the club," he told her. The urge to get blind drunk nagged him with a vengeance. Kat had made a fool of him, and there was nothing he could do about it.

Chapter 25.   Kat

"It went well today, didn't it, Kat?" Tim had hardly stopped smiling.

"Are you sure your dad's pleased?"

"He said so, didn't he? You've got nothing to worry about." He put an arm around her, snuggling closer on her sofa.

"He hasn't said anything more about moving to a bigger factory unit."

"In due time," Tim said. "You've got to think of the baby now. You should move out of this freezing flat, for a start."

"It's cheap," Kat protested. It was also within two miles of both the Jewellery Quarter, where Erik and Amy lived, and the city centre.

"It's cold, tatty and unsuitable. My place is too small, though. There's only one bedroom. I'll have to sell up and buy somewhere bigger."

His phone beeped. "It's a text from Angela. Look, Kat. She's sent congratulations and a link to a baby clothes website. How cute." He showed her the doll-like images on the screen.

It was as if her soul was drowning, swept beneath the waves of Tim's expectations. Kat yawned. "I really need to rest, Tim. Don't you have to be up early tomorrow to catch up on your sales calls?"

Tim took the hint. His blue eyes were sympathetic. "Good night, Kat. Sleep well. I'll call you tomorrow." He kissed her.

She waited, hearing Tim's footsteps on the rickety staircase, and the front door below being opened and shut. Satisfied he was gone, she phoned her brother.

"Kat, it's 10pm. What's up?" Erik asked.

"I'm pregnant."

"Ah. Are you pleased?"

"No. I feel sick all the time, and confused. Can you come round?"

"Give me ten."

Kat brewed tea for him while she waited. She always walked to Erik's flat, a good half hour for her, but he'd be much quicker on his bicycle. A steaming mug was sitting on the table when he arrived.

Erik embraced her. "I'm sure this will work out, Kat. Tim's a decent sort. Does he know?"

"Yes, and he's delighted."

"And you're not? Is it Marty you're afraid of?"

"No. Marty's cool with it."

"I thought he'd be worried about the business," Erik said. "We need cash for our darria research. If you have time off, it'll have an impact."

"That's all covered," Kat said. "Tim and I came up with a plan for the business before we saw Marty."

"Then what's the problem?"

Kat burst into tears. "It's me. I'm not maternal and I pity the child. Our mother's hardly the best role model, is she?"

Erik held her tight. "Kat, your moral compass is much stronger than hers. And don't they say it takes a village to raise a child? With me and the Bridges family behind you, you'll be just fine."

Doubt still nagged her. In keeping this baby, was she making the biggest mistake of her life?

Chapter 26.   Ben

Ben loathed his trips to Belmarsh. The drive from north to south London took over an hour. Public transport might have been quicker, but he hated the contrast between passengers going about their everyday lives, and those with the downcast eyes and watchful faces of prison visitors. Approaching the car park, he felt despair seep from the brick walls and forbidding metal gates ahead.

He was early. Needles of January rain chilled him before he was allowed to enter the visitor centre. His phone, watch and other valuables were swiftly stowed in a locker before he joined a queue to be frisked and admitted to the visit hall.

The group was not a merry band: fidgeting, yelling at children and otherwise subdued. Stone-faced officers patted down guests slowly, grunting at those who foolishly tried to engage. Apart from glaring at a screaming baby, Ben himself didn't initiate any interaction. He showed staff his visiting order and passport, making no comment and receiving none in return.

Thankfully, the baby and its mother were taken to a family room. In the cheerless visit hall, Ben was directed to sit at a formica table. It was hardly Starbucks, but his chair was comfortable and there was a limited selection of refreshments on offer. He was considering buying a coffee, when a gate was unlocked, and he spied his father. Ben waved.

"It's been a while." Shaun stumbled forward, his blue eyes boring into his son's.

Ben was about to give his excuses. He'd been travelling to tournaments abroad. The email booking system for visits was like pulling teeth. As he opened his mouth, he was overcome by shock at his father's appearance. Gaunt didn't even begin to describe it. "You look terrible," he said.

"Thanks," Shaun said, his tone laden with irony. He lowered his voice. "That's my intention. I've been holding back on food for months. You know it's the only way I'll get out."

"In a box, you mean?" Ben asked. "You were angling for a transfer to hospital, but it's not happening, is it?"

Shaun's laughter was hollow. "I've done all I can," he whispered. "I've lost weight. I've given urine samples with blood in them. Don't ask me how. I'm showing all the symptoms of prostate cancer; handing it to the quack on a plate."

"What are they doing, then?" Viewing the state of his father, Ben found it impossible to believe his woes were entirely self-inflicted.

"Don't shout, son."

Ben realised he was attracting attention from the lags and visitors clustered around tables nearby.

Shaun continued. "They're doing nothing. Tracy's written to the Number One Governor, and Jens is pulling strings, but they're doing nothing."

The furrows in Shaun's forehead deepened. He seemed older, his eyes sunken, as if the life force within them was dimming. Ben leaned forward to clasp his father's hand.

A guard shouted at them. Both men retracted their hands, Shaun holding his palms upwards. Ben instinctively copied him.

"It's down to me, then," Ben said. "I'll make a complaint."

At least that wasn't breaking the law. Helping Shaun abscond from hospital would be, though. Ben shivered. He couldn't let his father down, not with the old man's nerves and strength fraying so fast.

His father stared at him. His expression was the one Ben had seen when he'd announced he was going to university and, later, when he'd told Shaun he made a living playing computer games. It was a mixture of incomprehension and contempt.

Shaun's lip twitched. "Good luck with that," he said.

Chapter 27.   Shaun

"You must be joking," Sidey Carr spat.

"Look, Mr Carr," Ed Rothery said, injecting a sneer into the name, "I don't have time to argue. There's an incident elsewhere, my colleagues and I are required to attend, and evening association is over. End of. Period."

"I want to ring my daughter," Sidey said. Hostility spilled out of his voice and into his increasingly wobbly body. He made a fist.

The lags behind him in the phone queue looked interested at first – prison life was so tedious that any drama was a welcome diversion – then turned restive as they realised they wouldn't be calling anyone either.

Shaun knew the real reason for his cellmate's defiance: he was drunk on hooch, freshly brewed from oranges and Marmite. It was inconceivable that Ed hadn't smelled it on Sidey's breath yet.

"That's enough," Rothery said. "You want to go on basic? Up to you. I'm telling you to get back to your cell."

As much as Shaun had lost weight, Sidey had gained it, and he was determined to throw it about. An angry drunk rather than a happy one, he eyeballed Rothery and swore at him. "I'll take you down," he yelled, nutting the officer.

Rothery put his considerable bulk behind a return punch. Three cons piled in before anyone could stop them.

With a ringing epithet, Shaun pulled them off the screw. He couldn't stand by; Rothery was valuable property. "It's not worth it," he shouted, cuffing and kicking the lags.

The commotion attracted a gang of officers. Sidey disappeared in a scrum, still swinging his fists.

"My eyes," Sidey complained. "There are lines in front of my eyes. I can't see properly."

Nor, it transpired, could Ed. "Take Carr to the segregation unit," he ordered, his voice muffled. A colleague had given him a tissue, which he was using to grip his bleeding nose. "Halloran, who else was involved?"

"I didn't notice, Mr Rothery," Shaun lied. The other prisoners had melted away to their cells.

"Why did you help him?" Sidey's unfocused eyes attempted to glare at Shaun. A crafty grin stole onto his bruised face. "He's in your pocket, isn't he? You own him."

"Don't be ridiculous," Shaun snapped. "You think I want a month in seg? No TV or phone calls?"

Sidey shook his head, then evidently wished he hadn't. "I'm seeing stars," he screamed as he was led away. "I need a doctor."

"Get back to your cell, Halloran," Ed commanded.

Shaken, Shaun glowered at him before complying. He was dead meat if anybody, con or screw alike, believed Sidey.

Once the cell door was locked, he sought out the plastic bottle that Sidey had hidden behind his pillow. The contents resembled murky dishwater and smelled of rotten fruit, the stench of a dustcart or marketplace once its traders had left for the day.

"To absent friends," he said. "The devil's brew." Pouring it into his mug and holding his nose, he drank a toast to freedom. When would it ever happen? At least, in Sidey's hooch, he had a ticket to oblivion. Ignoring the foul aftertaste, Shaun swigged the remainder.

Chapter 28.   Vince

This time, Vince had finally done it. The stakes were so high, he had no other option. He'd shaved.

Ruefully, he fingered his chin. Pallid, receding and acne-scarred, it wouldn't win a beauty contest. Schoolmates had once tried to bully him over it. As he recalled the occasion, his mind put the emphasis on 'tried'.

He completed the look with a grey bobble hat and spectacles. They were geeky, with thick black frames, bought from a pound shop as reading glasses. The prescription was the minimum on offer, its effect on his vision almost imperceptible. He donned chinos and a black Crombie overcoat as usual, a normcore winter uniform that was common to half of London. Thus attired, he visited a library.

He chose Leytonstone. It wasn't on his doorstep, but it was handy for public transport. Vince walked to South Tottenham for the Overground, his newly exposed skin freezing despite the weak February sunshine. There was a strong wind blowing, and he was grateful for the hat.

At the Overground station, he bought an unregistered Oyster card to use a couple of times before discarding it. He wouldn't risk his motorbike for this sort of trip, where he wanted to slip through London like a ghost, unnoticed by the authorities.

As anticipated, the library's PCs were fully occupied. Free internet access lured students and pensioners alike. Vince waited for a scruffy teenager to claim a pre-booked slot, then offered the boy ten pounds to yield it. Within minutes, he had the information he needed. Vince waved the boy back into his seat, leaving with a smile on his lips. Ed Rothery had come good.

So had Ben. Thanks to him, Vince had ten thousand pounds in untraceable notes around his body in a running belt. Shaun and Jon were more inclined to use stick than carrot, but Vince differed in his approach. He'd wield the stick, naturally, if he had to. It just wasn't his first choice. Ben not only agreed, he'd provided the carrot.

Vince bought another Oyster card at Leytonstone tube station. He was lucky that his quarry lived in Greenwich, a mile or so from Ed Rothery, in the environs of the old market. This was an easy journey from Leytonstone. Even the fuggy, overcrowded tube and DLR didn't dent Vince's enthusiasm. He was optimistic. What idiot would refuse such a large sum of money? Maybe five thousand pounds would be enough. He discounted the notion quickly, recalling what happened to those who double-crossed the Hallorans.

Night had fallen by the time he arrived at the cobbled street where Nicholas Jakes lived. Vince found the address, a plain, flat-fronted brick terrace. It was in darkness. Just to make sure, Vince rang the doorbell. Receiving no reply, he waited for Jakes.

A black Peugeot RCZ-R coupé clattered down the road, stopping in the shadows opposite. From it, a fair-haired man emerged, his black North Face windcheater zipped up to his chin. He carried a briefcase. While it was hard to be sure in the dim light, he appeared to fit the description Ed Rothery had given: thirtyish, lean, over-long hair and nose. Rothery had mentioned a black sports car too.

Jakes had his house keys in his free hand. They could be used as a weapon. He was alert, glancing around as a policeman might. His eyes alighted on Vince.

It was crucial to avoid alarming the man until they were able to speak privately. Vince shuffled away from the brick terrace, turning in time to see the key had been placed in the lock. Springing at Jakes, Vince shoved him towards the door. It opened, Vince's momentum carrying both men inside the house and onto the floor.

The door gave straight into a sitting-room, faintly illuminated by the streetlamp outside. Jakes began to grapple, lashing out with his feet. "Get out," he panted, clearly winded by Vince's weight on top of him.

Vince smelled sweat, cheap soap and expensive aftershave. Scrabbling to his feet, he pushed the door closed, pressing the light switch next to it. He let his arms hang by his side, ignoring the blows Jakes landed on his jaw and chest. "Dr Nick Jakes, I presume?" he asked.

"What if I am?" Jakes said, throwing another punch. His face, thin, suspicious and furious, was clearly visible now.

Vince dodged, aware that his own anger was threatening to overwhelm him. Tempting though it was to pound Jakes into a bloody pulp, he knew it would be a big mistake. All that careful planning would be worthless. Jakes wouldn't co-operate; he'd go to the police. Desperately, Vince willed himself to stay calm and persuade Jakes to listen. "I've got good news for you," he gasped. "Ten thousand pounds of it, to be precise."

The doctor's attack halted immediately. "What do you mean?" he asked. His voice wasn't as upper class as Vince had expected. It bore strong overtones of south London.

Vince rubbed his jaw. To his relief, nothing was broken. "You heard," he said, delving below his shirt and unzipping the belt. He flourished a handful of notes.

Jakes's brown eyes darkened. "I don't have drugs to sell. Sorry."

Vince hadn't considered the possibility. "Not drugs," he said. "A favour."

"I don't do favours for strangers," Jakes said.

"You can't use ten thousand pounds, then?" Vince said. "Fine. I'll walk out of that door with it."

The medic stared at him, his silence allowing Vince to hear the gentle hum of appliances elsewhere in the house. He took in the huge widescreen TV on one wall, an original painting on another, and the gleaming chrome and leather furniture. It was a small house, but Vince wasn't fooled by that. The posh shops and bars he'd passed on the walk from the DLR station told him this area was wealthier than Tottenham, West Ham, or even Ed Rothery's patch nearby. The car screamed of riches too. Everyone knew doctors were overpaid; perhaps ten grand really meant nothing to a man like Nick Jakes.

Jakes took a deep breath. "Who are you?" he said. "What do you want?"

"Call me Bob," Vince said, plucking an uncle's name out of his brain. "As to what I want? It's five minutes' work for you. Send Shaun Halloran to hospital."

"Who's he?" Jakes said, to Vince's surprise.

"He's one of your patients in Belmarsh."

"Oh, yes." Awareness dawned on Jakes's pointy features. "One of the lifers. I really can't help you, I'm afraid, much as I'd love the money. The simple fact is, I can't refer him to a hospital, because he isn't ill."

"He's got prostate cancer," Vince protested.

"Really?" Jakes said. "Mr Halloran lost weight. Officers on his wing reported his appetite was much reduced. There seems an obvious connection. True, he presented a urine sample with blood in it. At the same time, there was a fresh, bleeding wound on his wrist, which he claimed was caused by bedbugs. I don't even see the need to waste my

106

nurses' time by admitting him to the prison's inpatient facility, let alone a hospital."

"We've all heard about things like this being missed. There's no harm in checking it out properly. Anyhow," Vince said, trying not to show his exasperation, "whatever you really think of his medical condition, it's someone else's problem once he's in hospital, isn't it? You can't treat cancer in the nick; he'd have to go to a specialist at the QEH."

The Queen Elizabeth Hospital was local for Belmarsh; Ed had advised that prisoners were sent there, albeit with an escort and a mountain of red tape.

Jakes was beginning to look interested.

Vince continued. "With those symptoms, who'd blame you for referring him? There's no risk to you, just ten grand cash in hand, tax-free." He sighed. "No risk to you," he repeated. "But if you don't want it, I'm leaving." He opened the front door.

"Wait," Jakes said. "Perhaps I've been hasty. Visible blood in his urine could be flagging bladder or kidney cancer. That's more likely than a prostate problem. In any event, professionally, it wouldn't hurt to make absolutely certain. After all, he is quite a high-profile inmate."

Vince closed the door again. Just as he'd thought, the carrot had been enough. Marshall would be different, though, he reflected sorrowfully. No carrot could be big enough for the task he had in mind for the former MP.

Chapter 29.   Marty

"It's all about Kat," Amy announced.

"Pardon?" Marty said.

"The Starshine marketing plan." Standing next to Marty's meeting table, Amy pointed a remote control unit at one of the wood-panelled walls. It slid away to reveal a huge screen. A presentation slide appeared with a tap of her laptop.

"There's been a gin boom in the UK since 2009," she said. "Craft gins are leading the way. Sales have almost doubled year on year."

"What's that got to do with Kat?" Marty asked.

"Listen up, Dad," Tim said. "Amy's market research is really interesting."

Marty poured himself another cup of coffee with cream, and stretched back, feet on his desk.

"The most successful producers are those who tell a compelling story to the media," Amy said. "We think we can do it for vodka too. I ran tests with separate focus groups of gin and vodka drinkers, mainly young people living in urban areas."

"How much did it cost to ply them with booze?" Marty said, wondering when the bill would arrive.

"Nothing," Amy said. "It was an online survey. Everyone who took part went into a draw for shopping vouchers with aspirational brands. They earned an extra place in the draw if one of their friends took part. That's how I extended its reach cheaply."

"Clever," Marty said. He gave credit where it was due.

"A very small number would buy Starshine if they knew nothing about it. That rises to ten per cent of the vodka drinkers when they're given an amusing quiz. But once they see a video of Kat explaining it's her brand and her dream, over half of both groups want to try it."

"Craft vodka hasn't taken off," Tim said. "But we know it can, especially if Kat is the face of Starshine. She's up for it, too. Kat will do..."

"Whatever it takes?" Marty said. "You don't need to tell me, son. I know she's ambitious."

"There have to be safeguards," Amy said. "Although Kat wants to help, she's afraid Shaun Halloran will find out where she lives and send an associate to kill her. In fact, we encountered one of them in a London pub six months ago, but that seems to have been a false alarm."

Tim jumped to his feet. "You're joking, aren't you, Amy? Kat didn't mention it to me."

"She didn't want to worry you," Amy said. "We knew it was just a coincidence, because the man saw her and ran away."

"Calm down, Tim," Marty said. "I take your point, Amy. Kat can front the brand, but we won't take unnecessary risks."

"I've been talking to a couple of exclusive clubs in London," Tim said. "High-end places, who take Snow Mountain. They'd allow us to introduce Starshine to select groups of journalists in specially curated events."

"We'd all be there, but Kat would take the lead," Amy said.

"She wants to do it soon, before her condition shows," Tim said.

Marty chuckled. "I can understand that. She likes tight dresses. And swilling vodka with a baby on the way isn't a good look."

Tim's eyes narrowed. "Kat hasn't touched a drop since Christmas."

"It'll take a month to arrange, at least," Amy said.

Marty tried, and failed, to remember when his wife's pregnancies had been visible more than two decades before. Angela favoured lycra underwear when she judged her weight to be fractionally too high; perhaps she could give Kat some tips. "We're looking at March, then," he said. "Let's do it around Charles and Dee's wedding. We'll all be in London anyway."

That would limit the cost. If Amy was right, his vodka business would finally turn the corner.

Marty hoped it would be in time. Erik was deeply unimpressed at the darria research freeze. Would he wait a few months longer, or would he lose patience and begin seeking funds elsewhere?

Chapter 30.   Shaun

Shaun's day had been a blur: the early awakening as he was dragged from his cell, the journey to hospital with double cuffs, the introduction to a cancer specialist in this secure, window-less room. Then there had been the 'fainting episode'.

He'd claimed to be dizzy. After staggering a couple of steps, he'd flung himself to the ground, taking a cursing screw with him. Having ensured he landed badly, crunching his head on the floor, Shaun had lain completely still with his eyes closed.

It hadn't worked. Although no one doubted he was out cold, they hadn't removed his cuffs. After he'd played dead for an hour, though, the screw to whom he'd been shackled had got bored. They'd left him chained to a bed, naked save for underpants and a hospital gown.

Both officers who had brought him to the hospital must be standing guard nearby. They weren't in the room, but they were probably just outside it, earning overtime while they drank tea and looked at dirty magazines together.

The bed was more comfortable than the bunk he'd left, although his surroundings were overheated and reeked of disinfectant. He was hungry, which was his normal condition these days, but he was desperately thirsty too.

It had been quiet for a while. Shaun cautiously raised his eyelids a fraction, allowing himself the merest sliver of vision. The small, square room was empty.

As his eyes adjusted to the blazing fluorescent light, he noted white walls, a white ceramic sink and a light wood door with an L-shaped handle. A plasticky blue curtain sectioned off a corner of the room. In size and institutional feel, the space resembled a very clean and modern prison cell.

There was the sound of a key in a lock. The L-shaped handle began to rotate. Shaun lay motionless.

Kat entered the room.

Was he dreaming? Because he'd pretended to faint, Shaun had received nothing to eat or drink all day. While he was used to short rations, he was hungry and lightheaded by now. Perhaps he was genuinely ill.

Uncertain if the striking blonde was a delusion, Shaun held his breath. Kat approached him, her long hair tied in a ponytail, an enquiring glint in her green eyes. She looked real enough. What was she doing here, in a nurse's blue tunic? Was that a syringe in her hand? Did she intend to kill him?

Feverishly, Shaun's glazed eyes stared at her, willing the apparition to disappear.

The news from Sidey's daughter was that Kat was making vodka in Birmingham. If she came to London, it would be for a drinks industry event, not to help the hard-pressed NHS.

As the girl neared, Shaun smelled antiseptic and alcohol rub rather than Chanel. Her chest hovered above him. 'Megan Plummer, nurse', Shaun read. It wasn't Kat.

Once he knew, he noticed differences: a shorter nose, an upturned mouth, a brisker manner. He chanced speaking, taking care to slur his words. "I'm in heaven," he murmured. "You're an angel in blue."

The nurse looked surprised, but not displeased. "Heard that before," she said, her vocal chords lower and less aristocratic than Kat's cut-glass tones. "I'm glad to see you're awake, Mr Halloran. I'd better let your escorts know."

"Escorts? Their private lives aren't my business," Shaun said. "Don't tell them anything, Megan." He deliberately used her name to establish rapport. "Look at me, all chained up in a locked room. I'm not going anywhere. My name isn't Houdini."

He paused. "It's not Mr Halloran either. I'm Shaun, darling."

Megan appeared to be stifling a giggle, but it emerged regardless. "Very well, Shaun Darling." She peered at him. "How are you feeling?"

"Could be better," Shaun said. "I've got the worst headache of my life, and I feel sick. I can't even move." He kept his limbs still, his iron will curbing the twitchiness imposed by lack of nicotine. Adding symptoms of concussion and stroke to his list of woes might stop the medics returning him to Belmarsh.

Megan regarded him with concern. "How's your vision, Shaun?"

"Blurry," Shaun said. "I can see lines and stars." That, after all, was what Sidey had yelled as he was carted away to the segregation unit.

Nobody had noticed that Sidey Carr was having a stroke. He might not even have been drunk. After he'd fallen over a few times, the screws had realised he wasn't kidding. Ironically, Sidey had been taken to hospital. Some guys had all the luck. Shaun had suffered months of dieting, when all you had to do was pick a fight with a screw.

Megan tutted sympathetically. "Has this happened before?" she asked.

"Just now, when I went unconscious," Shaun said.

"You've been through the wars," Megan said, scanning the notes clipped to his bed in a plastic wallet. "Suspected renal tract and prostate cancer. And fainting, of course. Let me take your pulse, please, Shaun." She placed a clip on the tip of his index finger.

Shaun felt a thrill as a beautiful woman touched him for the first time in three years, albeit to carry out a routine medical procedure.

"Now your blood pressure," Megan said, strapping a cloth cuff around his left arm.

"I can't feel anything in that arm, Megan. Or my left leg. I think it's a stroke." It was a challenge making his words sound garbled, yet sufficiently coherent and tinged with worry to raise unease in her mind.

"I'll put it on your right arm, then."

She switched it around. He felt the armband tighten and release.

"That seems normal," Megan said. "Are you ready for my party piece?"

"What's that, Megan?"

"A rectal examination. You can be sure I'll enjoy it as much as you will."

Shaun spluttered. "Is it really necessary?"

"It's absolutely standard. You had one at Belmarsh, didn't you? Your notes say they found an enlarged prostate in March – that's earlier this month."

"Of course." He'd had no such procedure. Jakes must have pretended to have done it. "I don't see why I need it again."

Megan shrugged. "Doctor's orders, Shaun Darling. Bend over."

Huffing, he complied, clanking his shackles and doing his best to make his left arm and leg appear useless.

"Going in now," Megan said, rolling a thin plastic glove onto her right hand and squirting lubricant over it.

She stuck at least two fingers into his rectum. They were cold.

"Ouch," Shaun complained, as she poked and prodded him.

"That's odd. I couldn't find anything," Megan said, withdrawing her fingers. She removed the glove and threw it in a bin. "I expect the consultant will try it himself. A second opinion won't hurt."

Shaun didn't agree. Still, the more work the medics had to do, the longer he'd stay. "I'm sorry you had such a horrible task, Megan," he said.

"All in a day's work," Megan said. "It's over to the doctors now. The next tests are above my pay grade."

"What sort of tests?"

"I expect they'll hit your leg with a hammer," Megan said, to his alarm. It reduced only slightly when she added, "A small one. Then you'll be sent for scans – ultrasound, and possibly MRI."

She lowered her voice. "Now I want to know about you. You must be a VIP to merit that level of security." She jerked her head towards the door. "They tell me you're a Mr Big."

Shaun decided to have a laugh. "Right. I rule the East End. On first name terms with the Kray brothers." He displayed a jauntiness he didn't feel. He'd never met the Krays, who were thirty years older than him and long dead.

Megan didn't seem fazed, just rushed. "I have to go," she said. "If your condition worsens, press this button, okay?"

"Listen," Shaun said, "I don't want to die here alone." He concentrated on memories of his wife until, finally, he manufactured a tear. "The screws – guards – won't tell my sons until it's too late. Do you have a phone on you, just so I can ring my eldest?"

"Sorry, it's in my locker," Megan said.

She was probably telling the truth. There were no bulging pockets in her uniform. Shaun tried again. "Then when you come off shift, please could you call or text him, just to let him know I'm here?"

There was a risk that his subterfuge would be discovered and he'd be hauled back to Belmarsh before Ben took the message, but Shaun thought the wheels within the hospital would turn slower than that.

"My son's called Ben," he said. "He's a good lad, not like me. He works in IT." There was no point expanding further: what girl would be impressed by an uber-geek? "You've got a pen, haven't you, Megan? I can give you his number." Thankfully, he could remember it.

Had he persuaded her? Nurses were trained to be caring, weren't they? Although similar in looks, Megan's personality couldn't be anything like implacable, hard-bitten Kat's.

"Tell him he needs a PVO. He'll know what that is – a prison visiting order," Shaun added.

"Okay, Shaun," Megan said. "I've got all that. Give me your son's number. I'm on my break in ten minutes."

A triumphant smile played on his lips as he watched her go. Even if she changed her mind, he'd find someone here who would help him. What cleaner or security guard couldn't use extra cash? Somehow, he'd get word of his location to Ben; then his son would do the rest. Shaun would taste freedom at last.

Chapter 31.   Vince

Marshall Jenner flatly refused to help.

"I'll go to the papers," Vince threatened.

Marshall yawned, almost certainly for theatrical effect. "Do it," he said. "Who cares whether I had an affair with you? The whole world knows I'm gay. It's old news."

"What about your wife?" Vince said. "You said she wouldn't be impressed."

"So?" Marshall said. "She's heard worse things from better people, to steal a phrase."

"I'm a convicted criminal," Vince said, a fact he'd omitted to mention before. "GBH."

"I spent nearly a year living with cons," Marshall pointed out. "I can be expected to know a few."

"You don't get it, do you?" Vince said. He aimed a punch, only to find himself sailing through the air and colliding with the floor. Fortunately, the hotel room had a plush carpet. His ego alone was bruised.

"I took the precaution of learning judo inside," Marshall said. "I persuaded one of my young friends to teach me after one or two incidents. Better late than never. Didn't I mention it to our mutual acquaintance, Al Halloran? Fancy that. I can't think why not." His face, always florid, was redder than usual.

Vince scrambled to his feet.

"Don't try anything else," Marshall warned. "I should go to the police, but I'm going to give you one more chance. I'm speaking in confidence to my lawyer, though. If anything happens to me, or anyone disturbs so much as a hair on my wife's head, you'll face all the retribution the law can throw at you. Understand?"

Vince nodded.

"It's a crazy scheme anyway," Marshall said. "Nobody can simply turn up out of the blue to see a prisoner in hospital, not even an MP. Which I'm not, thanks to what our legal system laughably calls justice. I can't believe Al had anything to do with your dubious plans."

Vince was silent.

115

"That says it all," Marshall said. "Well, thank goodness he's having medical treatment. I hope it succeeds." His eyes no longer twinkled with amusement. They oozed contempt, as he barked, "Get out."

Vince admitted defeat. Annoyingly, the room's soft-close door didn't permit him to slam it as he left. He slunk out of the hotel into the March sunshine.

It was another upmarket establishment, close to the Thames in Westminster. Marshall's wife was to join him later. They were attending a wedding there, and Marshall said they'd chosen to make a short break of it. Vince couldn't imagine why they should do so. They could as easily take a cab from Hampstead. Vince considered finding out where Marshall lived and trashing his house while the couple were away. An uneasy sense of caution stopped him. Marshall's threats were ringing in his ears. He didn't know what security arrangements were in place, or if anyone else would be there. Better to wait, and serve up revenge to Marshall later.

Gloomily, Vince wandered along the Victoria Embankment, staring into the steel-grey Thames. The sun had slipped behind a cloud and a sharp wind was whipping up the water. How much longer could he continue as the Hallorans' lackey? He should take whatever money he could from Ben, party hard with it and throw himself into the river's deadly embrace. Shaun could return to Belmarsh to rot, as far as he was concerned.

Then Jon's blue eyes flashed into his mind, remorse and clarity following. Despite the viruses drifting like aliens through his bloodstream, he'd never felt better. His beard was also recovering, albeit not as luxuriant as it had been before his visit to Dr Jakes. Jon would be out in a year, and still found him attractive. Until then, Vince could easily hook another sugar daddy. He didn't need Marshall Jenner's cash or company.

If Marshall wouldn't deliver a gun to Shaun, Jerry and Scott would have to spring him. Within the small band on whom he could rely, they were the only ones whose association with Shaun was unknown to the police.

Vince phoned Jerry at once, afraid the hospital would return Shaun to Belmarsh if he delayed. "I've got an urgent job for you and Scott. We'll have to plate up your van."

Jon had a relative, a mechanic, who could arrange false number plates. It was a simple matter to clone a Transit; there were so many of the white vans around.

"We're off to Bruges tomorrow morning," Jerry complained.

"Cancel it," Vince said. "This is more important."

"What is it?"

Vince explained.

Jerry was unenthusiastic. "I don't like violence. And Scott won't want a house guest. His girlfriend will do her nut."

"He'd better deal with her then," Vince said, suspecting more readies from Ben would oil the wheels. When he'd secured a promise from Jerry to locate Scott and meet in two hours, he sent Ben a text.

Ben phoned back. "I've got a PVO for a hospital visit tomorrow morning, but it's too late. They won't keep him in once they've done their tests and know he's faking it. You've got to get him out tonight."

"That hospital's massive," Vince said. "Which ward is he in?"

Ben sounded strained. "I don't know, exactly. I'm going round now for a recce."

"Better make it a good one."

Their success depended on Ben. It was lucky Shaun had no idea.

Chapter 32.   Marty

The hotel was upmarket and central, sandwiched between the north bank of the Thames and the ministries of Whitehall. Its spacious lobby was busy with guests checking in, porters pushing luggage trolleys, and smartly dressed individuals sitting alone. As others joined them, they disappeared towards the bar or restaurant. Marty was sure he recognised a politician or two.

He answered his mobile's ring without looking. "Where are you?" he asked. He'd been waiting ten minutes for Amy to emerge from her room. She was only supposed to be picking up a case of vodka samples.

"Pardon? Marty, it's Grigor."

"Good to hear from you again. It must be nearly midnight where you are."

"It's later than that," the engineer said. "Listen, I've had a long day." He stumbled over the words, evidently well-refreshed.

"And a long night, by the sound of it."

"I needed a drink," Grigor admitted. "I told you I'd lose my job over this methanol problem, even though nobody could have prevented it. It was an act of sabotage."

"It was the quality inspector, wasn't it?"

"Yes, with a trainee engineer. Both women. Nobody knows why. Marina thinks one of her husband's bastards was behind it. The police spoke to Anatoly Aliyev, but they didn't arrest him."

Either the truth was more complex, or Harry Aliyev's son had bribed the Bazaki police. They weren't noted for their tenderness. "What do you think?" Marty asked.

"I suspect revolutionary elements. We've had troublemakers at the distillery before. This time, they nearly poisoned the President. We made that vodka for the distillery's anniversary party, remember."

"I'm sorry to hear you're the fall guy," Marty said.

"At least Marina kept me on until today. I just wondered if there were opportunities in your organisation."

"I wish I could help, but I'm not recruiting at the moment." Quite apart from hassle with visas and work permits, Marty wanted a clean break with the distillery in Bazakistan. The contamination hadn't been Grigor's fault, but Marty couldn't risk any link with it, however tenuous.

"Maybe a maternity cover?"

"You've heard?" Marty said, surprised.

"People talk in our industry. Marina Aliyeva was overjoyed at news of a grandchild."

"I bet." If he didn't know Kat detested her mother, Marty could almost believe the two of them had planned it. "It's a long time before the baby's due, and Kat's only going to be off work for two weeks. She's training her team to cover for her during that time."

"I understand." Grigor sounded philosophical. "The passion for vodka is in her blood."

"Good luck. Listen, I've got to go. I'm in London on business."

"Thanks. I'll leave you in peace; I need some sleep."

The call vanished from the phone's screen. Marty looked at his watch. Where was Amy?

"Sorry I'm late, Marty."

He turned around. His marketing manager was dressed for a night out, in a sky-blue bare-shouldered top with ruffled sleeves. She'd applied scarlet lipstick to contrast with her coppery hair. Her wide black trousers reminded him of the loon pants he'd seen on older lads in the 1970s.

"Hello up there," he said, noting that, in stiletto heels, she was taller than him. "Forgive me if I've made a mistake. I thought we had business meetings to go to."

"They're in nightclubs. Kat told me to dress up," Amy said. "She's messaged to say she's running late."

"She's with Tim, isn't she?" The couple were staying in another hotel. Marty could guess what they might be doing. He preferred not to think about it. "Tell her we'll see them there. Our Uber's outside."

Their first destination was an exclusive, members only nightclub in South Kensington. The mirrored silver door was locked.

"I'll call the manager," Amy said, fishing an iPhone from her shiny black handbag. "Hello, it's the Starshine team. We're waiting outside."

Marty took an immediate dislike to the manager's old Etonian accent. Finn Branwell, a slim youth with short dark hair and beard, was otherwise unremarkable. He wore a black suit which, while obviously cut from an expensive soft wool, was little different in style to Marty's.

"We only open at nine. There should have been someone on the door for early guests. I do apologise," he said. "I've reserved our VIP area for you. It's a mezzanine overlooking the dancefloor."

"It'll be too loud to talk," Marty complained.

119

"Not at all." Finn's patrician tones were soothing. "We'll keep the music low until the club opens. That's what we agreed, right, Amy?"

She nodded. "Yes. The presentation will have finished by then. It's seven thirty now. The journalists arrive at eight. They'll be given cocktails."

"Made with?" Marty interrupted.

"Snow Mountain, of course," Finn said. "It's the best-selling brand behind our bar."

"Glad to hear it," Marty said. He began to warm to Finn.

"Kat will give a short talk about Snow Mountain and Starshine," Amy continued. "We'll have a tasting. We'll be done by ten to nine."

"You've got the VIP suite all night," Finn said. "I've allocated two staff to mix and serve your drinks. I just need to take your credit card details."

"That won't be necessary," Marty said. "We have to go on to another meeting at ten."

Amy frowned. "The journos might stay."

Inwardly wincing at the expense, Marty gave in gracefully. "How remiss of me. I'll sort that out now, Finn."

While he did so, Tim and Kat turned up, he in a suit and she in a tight black dress and spiky heels. Her figure betrayed no sign of pregnancy. If only it was a figment of his imagination.

Marty flicked the thought away as a tray of cocktails was delivered to the group. These had been cleverly mixed to reveal three layers of colour: red, blue and purple. Amy and Tim immediately helped themselves, while Kat declined.

Kat and Finn pecked each other's cheeks. This was a nightspot she'd frequented when she lived in the capital. She was on top form, greeting each journalist and plying them with drink as soon as they arrived.

There were six of them. The two drinks writers, men in their forties, reminded Marty of his beer buddies back in Birmingham. He guessed the four lifestyle correspondents, a slim and trendy man and three even thinner girls, were half his age. Each wrote for a magazine or newspaper read by millions of Britons.

"Shall we get started, then?" Amy's voice was as bright as her lipstick.

"Has everyone got a drink?" Kat beamed at the expectant faces around the circular, mirrored glass table.

There were nods and smiles. The rainbow cocktails were half-drunk, their layers blended to a vibrant magenta.

"Great. Well, I've introduced myself to each of you already. I'm Kat White, and this is my mentor, Marty Bridges."

Marty swallowed his shock. Kat wasn't sticking to the script.

"I first met Marty as a toddler. My father owned a vodka distillery in Kireniat, Bazakistan. I'm told that when this handsome English stranger visited, I hid behind my father's legs."

"Which handsome English stranger would that be?" Marty asked, coaxing a laugh from the drinks writers.

"My father and Marty developed Snow Mountain vodka, renowned for its purity. It's excellent in cocktails. You're drinking it now."

"I've been a fan of Snow Mountain for decades, as you know," one of the older men said. "You've started making it in the UK within the last year. Tell us more about that."

"My father's no longer around, and it was time for the next generation to get involved," Kat said, neatly side-stepping Harry Aliyev and Marina's recent ownership of the distillery. "I was educated in England and have made my home here, so it made sense to move distilling to Birmingham with me."

"Kat will tell you about Starshine, our exciting new vodka," Amy said.

"Yes, I want to continue my father's legacy, but I also had a vision for a brand I could call my own," Kat said.

The younger journalists murmured approvingly.

"It's completely different from Snow Mountain. That's a very clean grain spirit. Starshine is made with potatoes."

Tim spoke for the first time. "It's soft and creamy, and beautiful just on its own."

"Which leads naturally to trying a shot or two," Kat said. "Amy's pouring both vodkas for you, so you can compare them."

"There's a full bottle of each in your goody bags too," Tim said.

"Any questions so far?" Kat asked.

"Yes, what's your number?" the young man asked.

Kat handed him a business card. He scanned it into his phone. Their exchange was greeted with laughter by all except Tim, Marty noted.

Shot glasses were drained and replenished.

"I prefer the old Bazaki Snow Mountain to either of these," one of the girls said.

She wouldn't like it with a methanol chaser, Marty thought bitterly.

"Starshine's the best vodka I've ever had," the young man said.

He seemed persuasive. Within minutes, the others agreed with him. All six asked Kat to check her diary for interviews and photoshoots.

"We must go, I'm afraid," Marty said. "Feel free to stay at the club all evening. It's on us."

"Finn will look after you," Kat said, air-kissing him goodbye.

It turned out that the lifestyle correspondents were committed to at least two more parties each that evening. They slipped away, goody bags in hand. The drinks writers also took the half-empty bottles.

"We're meeting bloggers in Kings Cross next," Amy said.

"Well done, Kat," Tim said.

"Yes, good work." Marty could hardly disagree. Starshine, and Kat, appeared to be taking London by storm. His fortunes were bound to hers, whether he liked it or not.

Chapter 33.   Shaun

A scream cut through Shaun's slumber.

"Shut up. Not a word, or you're dead." It was Jerry's voice.

"What the…" Shaun rubbed his eyes as light flooded into them.

"Shaun!" Jerry, his face obscured by a fake moustache and dark glasses, wore the crested black shirt of a hospital security worker. He was pointing a pistol at the prison officer sitting next to Shaun's hospital bed.

Shaun had been shackled to a guard since he'd seen Nurse Megan. This screw's plan to earn easy overtime pay had gone horribly wrong for him. He looked terrified, and so he should. As far as Shaun knew, Jerry had never handled a gun before.

It started to make sense to Shaun. Elation bubbled within him, but not enough to stop him grumbling to Jerry. "It's about time. Have you got bolt-cutters?"

"For the cuffs? I've done better, innit? I've got keys." A shorter figure, similarly disguised, appeared in the doorway. It took him several tries before Shaun was unshackled.

Swinging himself off the bed, Shaun grabbed the handcuffs and applied them to his jailer. "What about the other one outside?" he asked.

"Tied up," Scott said. He jerked a thumb at the cowering screw. "His turn next."

"Can you keep the noise down?" Jerry hissed. "It's bad enough having this scum yelling his head off."

"I'll gag him," Scott said, stripping a pillowcase from the bed and stuffing it in the screw's mouth. He reached under his shirt and unwound a length of rope coiled against his belly.

"You're still a fat bastard," Shaun said.

"I'll do that," Jerry said to Scott. "You take the gun." He handed over the weapon.

Scott pocketed it. "I'll bring the other screw in here. We don't want Security finding him."

They had arrived just in time. The hospital had worked on Shaun faster than he'd expected. He'd had another rectal examination, MRI scans, blood tests and heart monitoring. "I have to hand it to you guys," he said. "You were there when I needed you. I reckon the quacks would have sent me back to the nick tomorrow."

He guessed the Number One Governor in Belmarsh had picked up the phone to the hospital administration. It must have cost a fortune in overtime to have two shifts of screws twiddling thumbs in or near this little room. How happy they must have been to earn extra money. Now it was payback time.

The prone figures on the floor were strangers, officers who worked on other wards. He didn't know and had hardly spoken to them. Nevertheless, all his frustration with Belmarsh spilled over as he kicked the bound and gagged guards, aiming for their faces and groins.

"Shouldn't we get going before Security come round?" Jerry said, as Shaun began to stamp on a screw's head.

"Okay. Lock them in," Shaun ordered.

Scott fumbled with a set of keys. "Can't find the right one, boss."

The medics probably had custody of it. "Don't bother looking for it. We'll close the door on them." Shaun was exhilarated, almost dizzy with relief. He punched the air with a newly-liberated arm before racing out into the corridor.

Jerry led the trio down the stairs and through a fire door into the car park. An alarm sounded as the chilly air assailed Shaun.

"Hurry up!" Panic mingled with the adrenaline coursing through him. He was wearing a thin hospital gown and his feet were bare, feeling each tiny stone as he scrambled over the tarmac. It hadn't occurred to him to look for his clothes and shoes when they fled; his sole focus had been running fast, and far away. "Got any threads?" he asked.

"In the van," Scott said.

In the middle of the night, the parking area boasted plenty of empty spaces. Jerry's white Transit shone like a beacon of freedom among them.

"Jump in the back," Jerry said, unlocking the vehicle. "There's cushions."

Shaun clambered inside, noting the jeans, jumper and shoes that had been left for him. There were also three garishly patterned bean bags on the cold metal floor. Apart from that, there was no evidence that the van, usually stacked with crates of booze, had been adapted to carry people.

He struggled to pull on the clothes, realising they belonged to a shorter and fatter man. "They're yours, Scottie, aren't they?" he said.

Scott cackled. "We were in a hurry." He seemed to realise it was hardly a tactful answer, if truthful, and said, "We'll buy you new ones."

The shoes pinched. Shaun took them off. He made himself comfortable on the bean bags as best he could, envying Jerry and Scott their seats in front.

Jerry started the engine. The van bowled forward, throwing Shaun onto the hard floor. He yelled, his swearing degenerating mid-syllable into a scream.

"I haven't even taken a corner," Jerry moaned, addressing the issue with a sharp left turn.

Shaun was pitched in yet another direction. With loud complaints, he endured a dozen similar episodes as Jerry swung the van into what appeared to be a maze-like warren of streets. "Where are we?" he shouted.

"Charlton," Jerry said, bringing the van to an abrupt halt.

"Small timers," Shaun said, with all the contempt a West Ham fan could muster for a football club two divisions below.

"You can get out now," Jerry said. He stepped down from the driving seat, opened the back door and handed Shaun a pair of sunglasses and a flat cap. "Hop in the front and sit in the middle."

Shaun did as he was told, noticing they'd stopped in an ordinary suburban street. A terrace of mid-century brick houses rose on one side of the narrow, winding road, and a wall on the other. Dim streetlights revealed no sign of life at this quiet hour, other than Jerry sticking another set of numbers over the van's plates.

"You should've done that before," Shaun snapped.

"Relax," Jerry said. "The others were fakes too. I'll drive over to your cousin, Clive, later, and he'll put new ones on."

Shaun understood Jerry's reasoning now: the bootlegger didn't want his van tracked across London, and he'd just rendered it invisible again. Still, after the battering he'd taken in the rear of the vehicle, he wasn't going to apologise to Jerry. "You got any fags?" he asked, as Jerry and Scott removed their shades and facial hair.

Jerry's left hand dived into his pocket. "I bought these in Belgium," he said, producing a packet of B&H and a lighter.

"Suppose they'll do," Shaun said, concealing his joy at smoking proper cigarettes rather than skimpy roll-ups. Old habits died hard, and he placed the pack and lighter in his own pocket after Jerry had lit a stick for himself.

The white van slipped out of the lattice of small streets, onto the main approach to the Blackwall Tunnel, and under the river. There was little traffic, save for the occasional milk float, taxi or supermarket goods lorry.

"What's the plan?" Shaun asked. He hoped there was one. Events had moved so quickly. He was unsure if Ben or Vince was in charge. Jerry and Scott certainly weren't.

"You're staying at Scott's," Jerry said. "We've got you a passport. Ben's sorting out a private jet to Marbella."

"Cash, no questions," Scott said.

The van emerged from the road tunnel. Jerry looped around towards Canary Wharf.

"Why are we going here?" Shaun asked. He saw signs for Millwall, and added, "That's another team with ideas above their station."

"They think they're so hard. We showed them in 1989, didn't we? Personally," Scott said, making a fist.

"Good times," Shaun said, nostalgic for the release offered by football violence in his youth. He nudged Jerry. "You're quiet."

"I'm driving," Jerry said, pointedly. "You wanted to know where. We're switching to a car at Canary Wharf."

"I'll take you back home," Scott said. "Jerry's running the Transit round to Clive in Canning Town."

"What do you drive these days?" Shaun asked.

"Same old. MX-5."

"I told him those Mazdas were hairdressers' cars. Will he listen?" Jerry said.

Shaun grunted, satisfied they'd have the horsepower to outrun the police.

They approached the complex of glass towers. Unlike the other buildings they passed, slices of light punctuated the dark obelisks, evidence of workers staying into the night. Jerry slowed at the entrance to the estate. A figure in a hi-vis cap and jacket materialised from a booth by the roadside.

"The filth?" Shaun whispered.

"Private security," Jerry said. He wound down the window. "I left some tools in my friend's car."

The stocky young man in his uniform, similar to police garb in shape if not colour, flicked his eyes over the trio. "Where is it?"

"Canada Square car park," Jerry said.

126

"All right." The youth looked bored. He couldn't be older than Ben. Shaun supposed he'd rather be playing video games than stopping vans on a murky night.

The Transit crawled through the clean, still streets between cliff-like buildings, overtaking a service vehicle. As the NCP entrance loomed, Jerry braked.

Scott jumped out. "I'll be five minutes." He disappeared past the barrier.

"We should be able to stop here at this time of night, no bother," Jerry said, but within moments, another of the security staff had appeared.

Jerry repeated the same excuse. This man was older and less easygoing. There was a terse debate, resolved when Scott's red sports car roared out of the car park.

Shaun exited the van. Scott held his passenger door open.

"What about your tools?" the truculent security guard asked Jerry.

Scott leaped out of the Mazda to present Jerry with a spanner. He made an ostentatious bow to the guard.

"You didn't want to do that," Shaun groused, once they were on their way. "He'll remember us."

"No, he won't," Scott said. "Trash like him attracts snark like a magnet. He's a jobsworth. Bet he supports Millwall."

"Now you mention it, he looks like a lad whose head I kicked in, back in the day," Shaun said.

"He deserved it," Scott said.

The short exchange seemed to have exhausted Scott's conversation, which suited Shaun. Edgy, almost speeding from lack of sleep and the urgency of the situation, he stared with new wonder at London's landscape. They returned to the jumbled streets of Poplar before skirting the old City of London to head north on the A10. The trendier environs of Shoreditch and Hackney soon gave way to the chicken shops and bookmakers of Tottenham. This was where young Jon had been forced to lodge in a humble flat when Shaun lost his empire. A twinge of guilt seared through Shaun's brain. He chided himself. It was Kat's fault; he must never forget.

The A10 bent away from the Tottenham High Road, heading through Bruce Grove towards the unexpected beauty of Bruce Castle, and suburbs beyond. Blue lights appeared in the rear-view mirror, and sirens wailed.

Shaun sat bolt upright, stomach knotted and fists ready. "Give me the gun," he hissed.

"It's an ambulance, boss," Scott said.

"No, it's the filth."

It was both. While the mirror showed an ambulance gaining on them, there was a stripy patrol car almost alongside.

"I'm going to have to pull over," Scott said.

"No," Shaun screamed. "Step on it." He tried to wrest the steering wheel from his rescuer.

Scott braked suddenly. The emergency vehicles sped past into the distance. Without a word, Scott accelerated, continuing their journey. Shaun discovered his hands were shaking, his ears attuned to the sound of absent sirens.

Signs announced that the A10 was now called the Great Cambridge Road. As Shaun glanced twitchily over his shoulder, London slipped seamlessly into Enfield, then the green fields of south Hertfordshire. Finally, Scott turned onto the slip road for the slumbering village of Broxbourne.

"Nearly there," he said, zooming through boxy modern estates and country lanes. At last, he arrived at their destination, parking on the brick-paved drive in front of his home.

Shaun had never visited the cottage before. He was city born and bred, uninterested in rural life. It was a relief to see that Scott's property stood in a large plot, well apart from its neighbours. To his discomfort, however, a light could be seen at the edge of a curtain in one of the windows that flanked the front door. "Who's the reception committee?" he asked.

Scott wrinkled his brow. "I guess Barbie's up," he said.

"Your girlfriend?" Shaun had never met her. Jerry and Scott weren't part of his inner circle. That made them especially useful now, however.

"Yes," Scott said. "I'll tell her to go to bed."

"You do that," Shaun said. "I'll have the gun too, please."

Scott reached into his pocket and handed it over, his eyes betraying unease. "Don't wave it around in front of Barbie."

"Then get her to behave." Shaun felt the smooth weight of the weapon, his fingers settling into familiar positions. It was a Glock 17 pistol, his favourite. He put it in his pocket. Still barefoot, he followed Scott as the bootlegger opened the front door.

The floor within was as cold and hard as the ground outside. Before Scott could flick a light on, a dog, barking with excitement, collided with Shaun's right knee and stood on his foot. He cursed.

"Down, Sooty," Scott ordered. He found the switch, illuminating the flagged hallway and a smoke-coloured greyhound.

"Nice dog," Shaun said, petting the animal's ears. He'd assumed it was a highly-strung breed, but it was affable enough. It stopped barking and regarded him with soulful brown eyes, reassuring him that he wouldn't need to shoot it.

The hallway was oak-beamed, with rosy pink walls. There was a galleried staircase and chunky oak doors leading to other rooms. The lady of the house made her entrance from one of these.

Barbie was unexpectedly taller than Scott, of rake-like proportions. She, too, looked to be in her late forties, which meant her cropped blonde hair must be dyed. She wore a long, fluffy blue dressing gown, and a sour expression. "What have you been doing all night? Who's this?" she asked.

"Barbie, Al. Al, Barbie. Al's an old schoolmate, here on business from Australia."

"A last minute thing," Shaun said, smiling despite the effort involved in adopting a fake Antipodean twang. "I've not been out there long. But long enough to miss the British ladies, though." He extended his right hand.

Barbie didn't move. Her gaze swept over him like a burst of acid rain. "Where's his luggage? Why's he wearing your clothes, Scott?" she sniped.

"A sad story of incompetent baggage handlers," Shaun said, fingering the weapon inside his pocket.

Scott noticed. Panic filled his eyes. "Al's just here for a day, or so," he said.

"Until I've bought a camper van to go touring," Shaun said. A hazy recollection told him this was what Australian tourists did.

"Until he's bought a camper van," Scott repeated. "Come on, love, hadn't you better go to bed?"

"Too right. I've got work to do in the morning," Barbie sniffed, stomping upstairs.

"I'll put Sh…Al in the spare room," Scott called after her.

"I want to call Vince," Shaun said. "Where's a phone I can use?"

129

Scott groped in his pocket, handing over a basic model. "Here."

"Thanks." Shaun glared at him. "I'll speak in private."

Scott took the hint and followed Barbie upstairs.

Shaun dialled Vince's number, one of a few hard-wired into his brain.

The phone rang for a minute before Vince answered drowsily. "How goes it, Scott?"

"It's Shaun. I'm at Scottie's. Wearing rags, but I'm on the out. How am I getting to the airport?"

"I'll be round in a minicab at ten thirty," Vince said. "Can make it later if you like; your flight isn't until the evening. It's going from Luton."

"Ten thirty's fine," Shaun said. "Can you get me clothes, shoes, a razor…"

"Got a suitcase all packed for you."

"Thanks," Shaun said, ringing off.

Scott reappeared, yawning. "Want to sleep now?"

"Spot on, mate."

The spare room turned out to be a boxroom on the first floor, a space not quite big enough for a bed and consequently filled with junk. Scott tossed a few cushions on the floor between a computer desk and a broken exercise bike. He added a blanket. "Sorry it's not luxurious," he muttered.

"Four-star hotel to me," Shaun said. Compared with Belmarsh it was. Still, he didn't wish to linger. It was obvious who wore the trousers in this household.

She was far too mouthy, but Scott clearly adored her. Her presence, and that of the gun, was eroding the trust between Shaun and his host. Scott would want to protect his happy home, but how far would he go? Would he attack a sleeping guest, or command his dog to do so? Worse, would he risk his own liberty and call the police?

Shaun couldn't sleep. He crept downstairs, looking for exits. At the back of the house, he found a kitchen, with a large window and a solid oak back door. Reassuringly, the key had been left in the lock.

He investigated the fridge. It was stocked with tofu, beansprouts and coconut milk. More promisingly, there were six bottles of strong Belgian lager at the back. He helped himself to one of these, and to oranges from a fruit bowl. Taking a knife and bottle opener from a drawer, he returned to his room.

Shaun left the scraps of the feast on the desk. Finally, he smoked two cigarettes in succession, grinding the butts on the perfect carpet.

Chapter 34.   Kat

"Ready for breakfast?" Tim asked. Freshly awake in the dawn light, he looked boyish: eyes wide, curls springing out at random angles without the wax.

Still in the mental fog between night and day, Kat yawned and stretched. A wave of nausea caught her throat. "You go ahead without me," she said. "I can't face it." She couldn't even bear to watch him eat.

"They do a full English downstairs," he said. "It always hits the spot."

"So you've stayed here before?" Kat asked. "I can't believe your father's nerve. He booked himself into a five-star hotel, and we're in the Kings Cross Travelodge."

Tim shrugged. "He's careful with the company's money. If it wasn't for Angela, he'd be here too."

"Sharing our room, to save even more cash?"

Tim laughed. "Go back to sleep, Kat. You had a busy night, and you need to save your energy for the wedding." He stroked her cheek. "I'll help you wake up later."

Bleary-eyed, she watched his naked body disappear into the bathroom. It would be a treat to spend time with him after breakfast. As Charles and Dee's ceremony wasn't until the afternoon, she could relax with Tim first. She snuggled under the soft white duvet to slumber again.

The previous evening had been hectic, unveiling Starshine vodka to influencers at two popular London clubs. Marty and Amy had left once the presentations were over. Kat, by contrast, had chosen to dance the night away with Tim at the second venue, a converted warehouse near Kings Cross. She recognised that Tanya had made a sensible choice in booking a hotel for them nearby. It was comfortable, but Kat was annoyed that Marty's lodgings were ritzier.

Anyway, being a couple of miles away, she wouldn't need to see Marty for breakfast. They'd never been friends, but she'd felt trust developing between them before Christmas. That was over, as if shutters had fallen on his jovial façade. While he was never less than polite, he maintained an emotional distance. He was taciturn with her, their contact limited to business meetings that he kept as short as possible. She hadn't been asked to join family gatherings at Wellington Road again.

Last night, when the East West Bridges team was invited to drink and dance as guests of the management, he hadn't wanted to linger. He'd even insisted Amy take a cab with him. To be fair, Amy had hit the vodka rather too hard, and she was staying in Marty's hotel. Marty wasn't paying for that, of course. Dee was picking up the bill, because Amy was a bridesmaid.

Clubbing had been fun without them, though, worth the blisters from stilettos designed for style rather than comfort. Kat's drowsy thoughts turned to the bridal celebrations later, a twinge of envy nagging her. She'd technically been married more than once herself, years before, but that didn't count. Each union had been a sham, arranged to help illegal immigrants to stay in London. Kat had received a thousand pounds a time for her trouble. She was lucky that Ross had paid for lawyers to set the marriages aside and to rescue her from a police investigation.

That was when she'd been engaged to Ross. Now, she couldn't imagine what she'd seen in him. He had looks and riches, but his personality was less than appealing. His apparent devotion had swiftly soured into selfishness. She'd found herself dressing and acting to please him, while he focused on pleasing himself.

Her relationship with Tim was different: she was an equal partner, rather than a pretty slave. She'd marry him in an instant, without an expensive party, if only he'd ask. As it happened, she still had the lacy white dress she'd worn as a fake bride in the past. Soon, her waistline would expand, and it wouldn't fit anymore.

Her pregnancy wasn't showing yet. If Kat ignored her sickness, her rejection of alcohol, and the tiny lump she could feel in her abdomen, she could imagine there was no baby at all. She wanted Tim, and the upmarket vodka business now, but the child still seemed to be an intruder, gatecrashing her life at least five years too early. Tim had persuaded her to keep it, but who did he really love – her, or the growing infant?

Perhaps it was both. She hoped so, holding the thought as she dozed through uneasy dreams.

Her phone rang. Groggily, Kat retrieved it from her bedside. She recognised Amy's number.

"You'll never guess who's on the front page this morning?" Amy's voice bubbled with energy.

"Dee?" Kat groaned. It was too early for guessing games.

Amy giggled. "You, in your slinky dress. We were papped arriving at the nightclub in Kings Cross. The rest of us were cropped out of the photo."

"No way." Kat allowed herself a grin. "Save me a copy, please." She'd have to start a scrapbook for press cuttings.

"Kat, why don't you come over and have your make-up done with the bridesmaids?" Amy said. "Dee's out doing a TV interview, so the rest of us are having champagne."

Kat was tempted, until she moved, and her morning sickness resurfaced. "I'm not drinking," she replied. She wanted Tim to return and deliver on his promise too. After that, why not? Pregnancy needn't stop her being sociable. She could reprise the old days, when she, Amy and their friends giggled together as they prepared to party in London on a Saturday night. Was it only three years ago? It felt much longer.

"I'll be round soon. Keep the coffee warm for me," she said.

Chapter 35.   Shaun

Shaun was woken by the sounds of trickling water and clanking pipes. He sat up, adrenaline jolting through him. Who was using his toilet? He'd had no cellmate since Sidey's departure.

Daylight filtered through flowery curtains, striking a wall decorated with butterflies in shades of peach. He was alone, as he should be, but not in his cell. Memories of the night flooded his brain: the dash to the car park, blue lights on the highway, the reception from Barbie. He grinned, then shuddered, glancing at the door. It was firmly shut, the exercise bike and other heavier items of junk piled against it.

Footsteps, and a television blaring into life, carried through the closed door as occupants of the house went about their morning routines. The plumbing wasn't located in the spare room, but it was noisy. Shaun moved the jumble out of his way, emerging onto the landing. His bare feet enjoyed the sensuous feel of carpet. He now recalled there was a bathroom opposite. Tiptoeing into it, his hand on the weapon in his pocket, he splashed his face with water from a pink sink. He dried himself with a matching fluffy hand towel, then used the blush-coloured toilet, deliberately leaving the seat up.

Downstairs, the boom of a television competed with the clatter of breakfast dishes. An aroma of scorched bread assailed his nostrils. Shaun realised how hungry he was.

He was supposed to be Australian, wasn't he? "G'day," he announced, entering the kitchen.

Scott and Barbie were sitting at a rough-hewn, rectangular oak table with two young people. A boy and a girl, they were both adult height, but had the spotty skin and diffident slouch of adolescence. They looked uncomfortable in their tight black school uniforms. Scott had no offspring to Shaun's knowledge, so these must be Barbie's.

The boy nodded, and the girl said, "Hello," before both returned to munching toast and staring at the screen that dominated the wall beside the door. Sooty lounged at their feet, catching the odd crumb as it fell to the floor.

Barbie's attempt at a smile emerged as a scowl. "Good morning, Al. This is Jack and Ashleigh. Sit down." She gestured to the chair next to Scott, a piece of heavy oak furniture like the table and kitchen units. "Would you like breakfast?"

She and Scott had bowls in front of them, in which Shaun spied half-eaten gruel. Evidently, bacon and eggs were out of the question.

"Hot buttered toast?" Shaun asked hopefully.

"Can do you brown, with Flora," Scott said, standing and removing two slices from a plastic-wrapped loaf kept within a wooden box bearing the legend BREAD. He dropped them into a toaster decorated with pictures of wheat grains.

"There's soy yogurt and fruit too," Barbie said. "Or coconut porridge. You're welcome to a bowl."

"No thanks, but a cup of tea would be nice," Shaun said, already nostalgic for a Belmarsh breakfast pack.

"I'll make it with soy milk and brown sugar," Scott offered.

Shaun nearly exploded. "How come you're so fat on a diet like that?" he asked Scott.

Barbie looked smug. "That's what I keep telling him, Al," she said. "It doesn't matter how healthy the food, if you eat too much of it, you'll put on weight." The television caught her eye. "Do excuse me; it's the yoga programme."

The teenagers immediately began studying their mobile phones. Barbie and Scott directed their attention to the screen. It held Scott's gaze even as he set Shaun's toast before him with a tub of margarine.

"Hi, I'm Dee." A beautiful woman beamed from the screen, brushing honey-coloured hair out of her face. She wore a tight red Lycra vest and leggings, an outfit which left nothing to the imagination.

"She's fit. Do you think those are real?" Shaun asked.

"I'd say so," Scott replied, so quickly it was obvious he'd already considered it.

Barbie fixed him with a glare that would have frozen hell.

"My gift to you today is a sixty second stretch," Dee said. "First, we're going to think of a beautiful blossom. Here's mine." She produced a daffodil. "Isn't it uplifting? Such a cheerful flower, filled with the scent of spring." She sniffed the bloom. "Don't do this at home if you've got asthma. Now, whatever you've chosen, just focus on it in your mind. Really appreciate the colour. Drink in the scent. Take a deep breath through your nose."

Shaun stared at the couple. They were breathing in, beatific expressions on their faces.

"Now, out through your mouth," Dee said.

Shaun was unimpressed. "What does a man need to do to get a cuppa?" he demanded, the Australian accent fading as irritation gripped him.

"I'll make one," Ashleigh said, rising to her feet and switching on a kettle.

At least one member of the household understood the meaning of hospitality. Shaun thanked her profusely, despite the tea's foul taste. He spooned extra sugar into it, vowing never to let soya milk near his tea again. Although he'd yearned for food during his low-calorie regime, he found he'd lost his appetite.

Scott and Barbie were kneeling on the flagstone floor, stretching their arms towards the ceiling. Dee, far more elegant, declared the exercise finished and told them to breathe once more.

"Strange. I thought you breathed automatically," Shaun said.

Barbie gave him another filthy look. "Be quiet," she said. "Dee's on the couch."

Shaun gaped at the television with renewed interest, only to see reality fall short of expectations. Dee was being interviewed by the presenter, a middle-aged man called Paul. He boasted an orange tan, obviously fake, unlike Dee's dewy glow.

"So, Dee," Paul said, "you're getting married today." He placed a hand on her arm.

Dee simpered. Her brown eyes sparkled. "That's right, Paul."

"And is this your first time?" Paul leered.

Dee confirmed that it was.

"I've tied the knot three times," Paul confided. "The triumph of hope over experience, perhaps."

Scott was fiddling with his fingers, clearly bored.

Barbie remained enthralled. "What a sleazeball. You tell him, Dee," she advised, as the yoga teacher said she wanted to be married forever.

"Mum, you're embarrassing," Ashleigh said.

On air, Paul complained he hadn't been invited to the wedding.

"It's close family and friends," Dee said.

"Like Kat White, the designer vodka queen," Paul said. "And Marshall Jenner, the MP who fiddled his expenses? You have some strange friends."

Dee giggled. "They might be my partner's buddies, Paul. Have you thought of that?"

Shaun wondered if his hearing was flawed. "Did she say Kat White?" he asked.

"They're good friends," Barbie said, giving every indication she was on intimate terms with Dee herself.

"Barbie teaches the same yoga moves as Dee," Scott said, with pride. "She's met Dee networking, haven't you?"

Barbie smirked. "Can't think what happened to my wedding invitation," she said.

"When is it?" Shaun asked.

"Keep up, Al," Barbie said. "It's today. Weren't you listening?"

Shaun clenched his fists. He'd have to take Scott aside and speak to him about keeping the woman in order. First, he needed Scott's help to obtain suitable clothes, not to mention phoning Vince and Ben. The sooner he was on that private jet, the better. It pained him that he had unfinished business with Kat, of course. She deserved to be punished for the long years he'd endured inside.

Maybe there was a way. He had a gun, and if he could only find out where Dee's wedding was, he could use it. The idea of revenge began to worry at him. Shaun was about to ask Barbie about the marriage venue, when he noticed the interview was ending. A hashtag appeared at the bottom of the screen.

"Viewers, you can follow Dee's happy day on social media," Paul said. "The hashtag is #yogadeeandcharles. Now for a summary of the news, starting with a report that's just come in. A violent murderer has escaped from custody in south London. Police are warning the public not to approach Shaun Halloran, who is armed…"

Before Paul could say more, Shaun spilled his tea. The tepid liquid covered the table in a sticky sheet, then dripped onto the floor. Sooty, the greyhound, started lapping up the puddle.

"Silly me," Shaun said, his fake Aussie twang more pronounced than ever. Somehow, in jumping to his feet, he was standing in front of the television. "Do you have a cloth?"

The dog slunk to the back door, whining. Either it detested soya milk too, or it had drunk enough to warrant a trip outside. Scott released it into the garden, then scrubbed the table and floor. The rest of the family stayed seated, Barbie pursing her lips. Shaun joined them again once he was satisfied that Paul had moved on to other topics.

"It's World Water Day," Paul said. "The theme is Why Waste Water? We'll be talking to schools in London about their efforts to save our precious aitch-two-oh."

That sounded dull to Shaun. Barbie evidently thought so too. She switched off the set. "Time you went to school," she told her children.

Shaun's sweaty hand reached into the pocket of the dreadful loose, short trousers, and clutched his pistol. He should shoot all four of them, and have done with it. It wouldn't take much for Barbie and the children to grasp the truth: a repeat of the local news on television, or a glimpse of a newspaper, and he'd be back inside.

The dog reappeared, worrying at a bone. Scott fondled its ears. Shaun felt sick as he saw a loving glance pass between his old schoolmate and the animal. Relaxing his grip on the weapon, he knew he couldn't kill Scott. This was one of the few men he could trust, a friend who had offered shelter in his hour of need.

The doorbell rang. "I'll get it," Barbie said, following the teenagers out of the kitchen.

Scott, still petting Sooty, tutted. "Another Amazon parcel?" he said.

Whoever was at the front door, Barbie wasn't keen on them. "You'd better come in," Shaun heard her say, her tone grudging. Moments later, she returned to the kitchen.

The first thing Shaun noticed was the two peaked caps her companions wore, the black and white chequered pattern as revealing as a flashing blue light. Momentarily, his hand gripped the Glock 17 again. Then, holding his loose waistband with his other hand, he rushed to the back door.

It was still unbolted. Shaun darted outside.

Sooty followed him, barking. The dog obviously thought it was a game. Shaun picked up a loose stick and threw it as far as he could. His ploy worked; the animal raced after it.

Scott's garden appeared to be an enormous lawn, almost the size of a cricket pitch. It was bounded by beds and shrubberies, and a fence the height of a man. Shaun ran in the opposite direction to the dog, scaling a fence on the right-hand side.

This gave onto another plot of similar size but with more shrubs and trees. The householder also liked rose bushes, as Shaun discovered when his bare feet landed on thorns. Sooty's barking, and the sound of men in Scott's garden, stopped him uttering curses.

139

Cradling the gun against his chest, he crept from tree to tree, using them for cover and navigating his way around the side of the house. At the front, he checked the roadway, left and right.

The only sign of a police presence was the patrol car parked on Scott's drive next door. Shaun bolted around a corner.

Ahead, the houses were newer and closer together than Scott's old cottage. Shaun dived into a less well-kept garden offering refuge in its trees and straggly undergrowth. Hiding behind a shrub, he saw one of the police officers dash along the road. Although the fellow was alert, flicking his eyes to both sides, Shaun had concealed himself too well.

Broxbourne would be crawling with the filth soon. How had they known? Shaun regretted his kindness in sparing the lives of Scott and his family. They hadn't deserved it. Desperately, he scanned the neighbourhood for a means of escape.

He saw a black Mercedes C class saloon on the drive of the house opposite. Its owner was just emerging from the house, opening his car with a click of the central locking.

Shaun sprinted towards him.

"What do you want?" The man's voice was refined, his body language solid. He was probably in his thirties, tall and slim, his mousy hair cropped close to a squarish head. His clothes, a charcoal suit and blue checked shirt, spoke of a day ahead in an office. The car bore a personalised number plate, PAT 72. This was someone used to getting his own way.

In a matter of seconds, Shaun took in his victim's height and build, and made his decision. "Do as I say, Pat," he said coldly, "and you won't get hurt. Give me the car keys." He flashed the edge of the pistol in his pocket.

Pat didn't hesitate. He placed the fob in Shaun's free hand.

"Now, get in the car," Shaun commanded. "In the driving seat."

Pat looked as if he wanted to argue, then appeared to think better of it when Shaun glared at the gun. He stepped into the car. His Adam's apple bulged against the top button of his shirt, his freckled skin flushing.

Shaun sat next to Pat, handed him the key, and ordered him to drive.

"Where?" Pat asked, his demeanour more submissive now.

It was a good question. Unfortunately, it was difficult to answer. All Shaun knew of Broxbourne was that it was on the A10. "Find a country field that's quiet," he ordered.

140

Pat trembled. "You don't need to kill me," he said. "I'll do everything you say."

"Good. Then I won't kill you," Shaun said. "But be in no doubt, Pat, I certainly will otherwise." He stroked the Glock 17, and kissed it. "This little baby never misses."

Shaun ducked down as Pat reversed off the drive, nearly knocking a policeman over. Pat shouted his apologies. The policeman seemed to know him and paid no further attention.

"I thought we could go to the river," Pat said.

"I don't need a travelogue," Shaun growled. "Just remember, I'm right here." He nursed his weapon in his lap, while Pat drove to the edge of the village.

The landscape switched abruptly from modern housing estates to green fields. The car ambled over a river bridge, turning shortly afterwards into a large car park.

"This doesn't look quiet," Shaun said suspiciously, eyeing a collection of low wooden buildings.

"Nobody's around," Pat said, anxiety increasing the pitch of his voice. "This is the country park. It isn't open yet. Now, will you let me go?"

"Not yet," Shaun said. Theirs was the only vehicle in sight, so Pat probably wasn't lying. "Stop the car, then."

Pat complied. "What do you want from me?" he asked.

"Get out of the car, and take your clothes off."

Pat made a gagging sound. Spittle bubbled on his lips. "My God. Not that, please."

"Are you calling me gay?" Shaun asked. He grimaced. "I'm not, so cut the hysterics. Just do as you're told." He added, "You can keep your underpants on." Waiting until the businessman was outside the car, he exited it himself. Holding out his hand, he said, "I'll have the car keys back, please. And everything in your pockets."

Pat extracted a wallet, driving licence, comb, iPhone, packet of Polo mints and some loose change. He placed them carefully on the car's bonnet, before stripping down to his boxer shorts.

The clothes bore Marks & Spencer labels. Shaun shook his head. In his heyday, he'd had his garments made for him in Savile Row. Still, he had no choice. With luck, he wouldn't catch any infections or infestations; no noxious odours floated towards him as Pat undressed. "Socks too," he ordered, removing his jeans with one hand.

141

Pat stared at him, animal fear in his brown eyes. "You said…"

"I'm not gay," Shaun shouted. Collecting himself, he said, "Tell me your PIN numbers, for your phone and your cards. Don't lie."

"4321," Pat said. "I use it for everything." He began to sob.

"Really?" Shaun said. "How careless. Anyone could guess that."

"You don't have to," Pat whispered.

"Thanks." Shaun smiled. "That's all I need from you, Pat."

"Then you can let me go. Please," Pat begged. "I've got a family. A wife, and a baby daughter. I want to see her grow up..."

"I have to be certain you won't talk," Shaun interrupted.

"You can rely on me," Pat said.

"I said, I've got to be certain, Pat. Sorry, mate." Shaun whipped the man's forehead with the butt of the pistol.

Pat staggered groggily backwards, falling to his knees.

Shaun found the boot release button. It wasn't difficult; he'd driven Mercs before. He risked putting the gun down as he hoisted Pat's semi-naked body in the air, thanking the gym work-outs that had built the strength he required for the task.

Pat didn't fight as Shaun squashed him into the car boot. The businessman didn't even groan when his knees and elbows were shoved against sheet metal.

Stuffing his jeans in Pat's mouth, Shaun closed the boot and dressed quickly. Pat's shoes were a size too large, but the suit and shirt only fractionally loose. Filling his pockets, Shaun adjusted the driving seat, switched on the satnav and set his course for the A10. He didn't yet know where Dee was getting married, but heading for London was a good start.

Chapter 36.   Marty

"Wake up, Marty."

Enjoying a dream in which he appeared to have hair on his head and an unlimited supply of beer, Marty resisted the call. Finally, he felt his shoulders shake. "S'earthquake," he mumbled.

"Wake up." Angela's manicured hands caressed his shoulders. She was wearing a baby doll nightie, in a sky-blue hue that reflected her eyes. Daylight, blurred by net curtains, lent her skin a soft glow.

The unfamiliar room, restful in creams and blues, swam into focus. He remembered they were staying in London, in the prestigious hotel where Amy's father would be married later. "What's the hurry, bab?" he asked.

"The hotel stops serving breakfast at ten thirty."

"What?" Marty shook off his languor and sat up. "I've paid for it. I want a full English, with extra smoked salmon, champagne and unicorn's tears for the amount they're charging."

"I thought you would," Angela said. "You've got an hour."

"No chance, then," Marty said. "It'll take you that long to do your make-up."

Angela played it with a straight bat. "It's just a light touch for me," she said. "A smidge of tinted moisturiser and five minutes for facial exercises." She demonstrated by slapping her chin and gurning in front of him.

His phone rang. Angela waved, disappearing to the ensuite bathroom with a well-stocked bag of toiletries.

"What news, Ray?" Marty was becoming increasingly used to calls from his bank manager.

"You've asked me to process an excise duty payment. I can't do it, Marty. You'll breach the overdraft limit."

Marty almost felt the last of his hair fall out. This shouldn't be happening. He managed the bank account carefully. One of his customers must have been late paying him. He didn't have time to investigate, but he couldn't afford to tangle with the taxman. "HMRC will close us down if that transfer doesn't go through, Ray. How about increasing the limit? My cashflow problems are temporary."

"This temporary problem has lasted for more than half a year. I'm sorry, I can't stretch the limit further without taking a charge on your house."

Marty sighed, glad Angela wasn't listening. "All right. If I email you now to confirm that, will you release the payment? We can sort out the paperwork later."

They reached agreement as Angela returned, skin glowing and hair freshly curled.

"Ready to tackle your hangover, Marty?"

"If only I had one, bab." He grinned, remembering the previous evening. "I prefer a pint to a vodka shot, but it seems I'm on my own. The journalists loved Starshine."

"Kat knows her stuff, doesn't she?" Angela said. "Vodka-making is in her blood."

"Sadly, that's not all," Marty said.

"You've got to stop viewing her in such a bad light," Angela said. "She's part of the family now."

"Don't I know it," Marty grumbled. "I don't need to like it." With the baby, Kat was tied to his son forever. She would be woven into the fabric of Tim's life long after she'd bled him dry and moved on to a more attractive prospect.

Chapter 37.   Vince

Vince's phone rang. He hoped it would be Shaun or Scott. The smile died on his lips as he saw Ben's number.

"Are you with Dad?" Ben asked.

"No," Vince said. "He made it to Scottie's last night, but it's been radio silence this morning."

"The police woke me up at 4am to search my flat. Three of them. They only just left, although it was obvious Dad wasn't here."

"How many empty pizza boxes did they move to work that out?"

Ben ignored the slight. "You need to get him to Luton," he said. "The flight's good to go at six o'clock tonight. I booked the jet over the dark web. It can't be traced to me."

Nothing could, Vince thought bitterly: not the mobile phone Ben was using, the money that was greasing open palms, and now the private jet hire. If it all went pear-shaped, he could guess who the lawmen would be chasing. Shaun Halloran's elder son would walk away, his halo intact.

"Passenger name is Trevor Finsbury," Ben added. "That's the passport you've got for him, right?"

"Scott's got it," Vince said. "I'll call him again. They're probably still in bed. It was a late one."

Once he'd said a less than genial goodbye to Ben, Vince began trying to rouse Scott again. Phone calls, texts and WhatsApp failed to bear fruit. He rang Jerry, who was back home in Ilford, unenthralled to be woken up, and didn't have a clue what Scott and Shaun were doing.

They'd agreed it was Vince's job to arrange transport to Luton Airport, and he did so by hiring a minicab from an outfit in Seven Sisters, far enough from his flat that he'd never used it before. He would have preferred to rent a van, but that required too many fake documents.

Walking to Seven Sisters down the High Road, past the jumble of kebab joints, bookmakers, phone shops and vaping parlours, he was struck by anxiety. Apart from the unease caused by Scott's lack of contact, he was carrying more cash than usual. His wallet held several hundred pounds to defray expenses, and there was a wad of euros in Shaun's suitcase. Vince had ready fists and a couple of knives about his person, but he missed the Glock 17 that he'd lent to Scott.

At the minicab office, they were happy to send a car to Luton via Broxbourne, as long as Vince paid in advance. They quoted three hundred pounds. He haggled the price down to two hundred and twenty, suspecting they would think it odd if he didn't try.

"It'd be cheaper for you on the train, bro," the driver cheerfully observed as Vince sat beside him in the car, an old Honda.

"I don't like trains," Vince said. It wasn't true, but all modes of public transport were bristling with cameras. Although he'd packed a wig and moustache, he couldn't be sure Shaun would agree to wear them.

The cab lurched from one traffic jam to the next. Vince started counting the sets of lights. He stopped at twenty. The train would have been quicker. It was a scenic journey, though, with plenty of green space even before they left London behind. The trees were just beginning to come into leaf. Vince stared silently out of the window, resisting the amiable young driver's attempts to chat. The youth was straight, in his early twenties, a Londoner of Greek Cypriot extraction living in Wood Green and studying part-time for an IT degree. This much Vince ascertained without either having any interest in or encouraging the lad to speak about his life. Like the forest pond's water, the stream of words washed over him. Eventually it ceased.

Without asking, the lad switched on the radio. Vince enjoyed the blaring dance music at first, but then came the news bulletin. Thirty seconds later, Vince heard police were seeking Shaun Halloran, a convicted murderer on the run. An alleged friend of the prisoner, a woman called Tracy, was quoted as saying that he was very ill and she feared he'd been kidnapped by rival gangsters. Vince had no idea who she was. He didn't wait for more, but said rather sharply that he had to use his phone, and could the noise be reduced, please?

Once they were through Enfield and into the countryside, roads were less clogged but the journey still wasn't fast enough. Vince alternately drummed his fingers with impatience, and jabbed at his phone in a vain attempt to reach Scott. Perhaps he was panicking for nothing. The police were still searching, weren't they? Nevertheless, Vince's disquiet grew as the minutes ticked by without word from Scott.

They couldn't afford to bungle this. Shaun inspired loyalty because he was a diamond to his friends, but equally, no one would wish to be on the wrong side of him. Rumours abounded, such that only a fool would believe the murder for which he'd been sent to Belmarsh was the single one he'd committed. His revenge when crossed might be neither swift nor subtle, but it would materialise as surely as the sun rose in the east.

Quite apart from the fear inspired by Shaun, Vince wanted to succeed for Jon. The younger Halloran had said Vince was the only one for him: there was no one else inside, even. Vince dreamed and hoped it was true. They'd be speaking tonight, and he wanted to tell Jon that it was mission accomplished, and Shaun was on his way to the sun.

His tension increased as the car slipped off the A10, through Broxbourne's newish housing estates, and towards the older part of the village. The church came into view, and Scott's cottage not long after it.

There were two squad cars on the drive.

"This is the place, yeah?" the young driver asked, slowing to a halt across the road. He turned to face Vince, suspicion written on his chunky features.

"No," Vince said. "I've changed my mind. Take me back to London." He could see a policeman standing next to one of the cars, starting to look interested.

"Wise move, bro," the driver said, heading further down the road and adjusting his satnav as he did so.

Silence cloaked the air. Luckily for both of them, the youth had too much sense to ask questions.

Vince texted Ben. The filth had caught Shaun. How much would they learn from Scott? His nightmare was happening.

Chapter 38.   Shaun

Shaun parked in a side street close to the Victoria Embankment. Grand white stone terraces, their facades adorned with balconies and curly carvings, lined both sides of the road. He huffed, supposing these were mostly government buildings, funded by taxpayers. He counted himself among their number, despite his best efforts to avoid paying any kind of levy to the government.

There were plenty of parking spaces, no doubt because of the signs that announced parking was permit-only. A quick glance at his windscreen told Shaun that Pat didn't have a permit. That, like the London congestion charge now due on Pat's Mercedes for entering the capital's centre, was someone else's problem. At worst, the Merc would be towed away, with Pat inside the boot.

It wasn't yet midday. Shaun had been busy since he hijacked the car. He'd acquired and donned dark glasses, before buying a length of rope, a cheap mobile phone on a pay-as-you-go tariff, cigarettes, a lighter and a burger with fries. The new phone had been charged in the car. Smoking furiously, he'd found a quiet spot to stop and bind his captive properly, Scott's fruit knife proving its worth in cutting the rope.

The wad of cash in Pat's wallet had been enough to pay for the goods. Pat's credit and debit cards remained untouched, while his iPhone had been used only for web searches. It took mere minutes to find out where delectable Dee was tying the knot.

The purchases, and the journey, were more time-consuming than Shaun would have liked. He could have taken a faster route, orbiting north London on the M25 motorway, before heading south to Woodford on the zippy M11. Woodford and nearby Wanstead were very familiar to him, and he knew exactly where to buy everything he needed. Unfortunately, the risk of recognition was too great. He was well-known in the eastern fringes of London. Instead, he had to content himself with the Great Cambridge Road and a large Enfield retail park. At least he'd enjoyed taking the wheel of a Merc again. The car behaved like an old friend, its leather driving seat fitting him like a glove.

Now, he sat in the car by the opulent hotel where Dee was to be married, indulging in another cigarette. Raindrops thrummed on the windscreen as grey clouds passed overhead. Shaun picked up the cheap, untraceable phone, and called Ben.

"It's me, son."

"Dad?" There was disbelief in Ben's voice. "Where are you?"

"Finishing some business," Shaun said.

"I thought…" Ben's voice shook. "Vince told me the cops got you. This isn't your single phone call, is it?"

"I wouldn't waste it on you if it was," Shaun said brutally. There were lawyers a lot more use than his unworldly son. His tone softened. Ben wasn't totally clueless. He was making good money playing video games, and spending it to help his father. "The filth came calling, but I got away. I've just got a little job to do, and then I'll be free to fly like a bird. Is the plane sorted?"

Ben breathed in sharply. "It's a private jet. The flight leaves Luton at six tonight. Where are you?"

Shaun ignored the question. "I can be there."

"You need a passport," Ben said. "Scott was supposed to give it to you. Has he?"

Shaun released a volley of curses. "No, I don't have it," he said. "Only a driving licence in the name of Patrick Mulligan."

"Does it look like you, Dad?" Ben asked.

Shaun examined it. Although a poor-quality photograph, Pat's mousy hair and blunt jaw were apparent. Anyone would notice the lack of resemblance. "No," he said.

"Vince and his friends will have to arrange a passport," Ben said. "We'll text you once that's done. Then we'll have to give it to you. It would help to know where you are."

"Text me with a meeting-place," Shaun said. "I've got wheels."

Although Ben replied, the answer didn't register at all. From the corner of his eye, Shaun saw a young blonde step elegantly out of a taxi, red stilettos lengthening her shapely legs. She was dressed for the changeable weather in a leopard-print coat cinched at the waist. The hood was pulled back to reveal red flowers in her hair, and a face that had haunted him for too long.

"Got to go, son," Shaun said. "I should have killed Kat before, and I'm not missing a second chance."

Chapter 39.   Vince

"He got away," Ben said.

"Hallelujah," Vince said. Relief surged through him.

"He hasn't got a passport," Ben said. "You'll have to get him another one. I'll rearrange the jet hire, but I need a name as soon as possible, okay?"

"I'm on it," Vince said. "It'll cost you." Jerry could persuade a friend to lose a passport. "Where's your dad?"

"I don't know, but I want to find out." Ben's voice was grim.

"Don't we all."

"He's going to kill that girl, Kat," Ben said.

"It's nothing to do with us." Vince neither cared, nor blamed Shaun for disposing of an enemy. It was what you did to make others think twice before discarding your friendship.

"He's putting the whole operation at risk," Ben said, sounding like a secret service agent.

"His choice," Vince said, pretending an indifference he didn't feel. The hairs on his spine prickled. Ben was right, albeit Vince suspected his motives. He remembered Ben chatting to Kat at the bar in Shoreditch. What had Ben said, that he only dated girls who played video games? That was so obvious a lie that Vince wished he'd challenged it. Straight men were incredibly predictable: Kat was the type they all fancied. In fact, that was why Shaun had employed her in the first place.

"How can I track him down?" Ben asked.

"Listen, Ben," Vince said, "You're the eSports star and king of hackers. If you can't do it, no one can."

Chapter 40.   Shaun

At his empire's zenith, flush with the proceeds of drugs and prostitution rackets, Shaun had frequented clubs and casinos in the West End. Their entrances were brash, with bright lights, buffed-up metal and marble steps beckoning to delights within. This hotel was nothing like that. Although a grand white building similar to others in the street, its doorway was modest, flanked by clipped box trees. There were no liveried flunkeys or even bouncers outside. Shaun wondered if this was the right place. Perhaps he'd hallucinated the image of Kat striding confidently through the door. There had been other times when he was convinced he'd seen her, hadn't there? He recalled a television programme about vodka, and his encounter with Nurse Megan.

Dee had invited Kat to her wedding, though, and the all-knowing Google said the ceremony was taking place here. Shaun took a deep breath, entering the door alcove.

As soon as he did so, his fears were dispelled. A short man of Mediterranean appearance and middle years, smart in tails and top hat, appeared from the side to open the door for him. "Good morning, Sir."

"I'm here for a wedding," Shaun said, relieved that Pat's Marks and Spencer suit had lent him respectability despite a couple of days' stubble.

"It's not until two o'clock," the doorman said. "There's a girl inside who can help you. Ask the concierge."

Inside, the lobby was a large white oblong space with an ornately carved ceiling. One end was occupied by the polished wooden desks of the receptionists and concierge, and the other by red velvet sofas where businessmen did deals over coffee.

The concierge directed Shaun to speak to a young woman sitting on a crimson velvet chair. Petite, wearing a red trouser suit, her black hair in a neat bun, she rose to greet him immediately. "Hi, I'm Emily," she said, beaming and shaking his hand. Her fingers felt smooth and cool. "And you are?"

"Marshall Jenner," Shaun said, betting that Emily would be clueless about Marshall's appearance. Even if she'd heard of Marshall, the ex-MP's notoriety wouldn't make him persona non grata; he was an invited guest, a friend of the groom, according to Dee's comments on breakfast television.

Emily's smile didn't falter. She tapped at an iPad. "Welcome to the celebrations," she said, "and commendably early too. In fact, drinks aren't set up in the room yet, so feel free to have a coffee in the lobby or a drink at the bar."

"Well, actually," Shaun said, "I have a message for one of the other guests, Kat White." He made an effort to speak with a plum in his mouth, as he remembered Marshall doing when they had shared a cell. "I saw her arrive earlier, but just missed talking to her, I'm afraid."

"Yes, she's with the bride," Emily said. "I can ask a colleague to find her and deliver the message for you, if you like."

"It's personal," Shaun said. Adrenaline flowed through him, pent-up energy ready to be unleashed. He was so close to her now. In a calculated risk, he took off his dark glasses, making sure to smile as he did so. The image he presented bore no resemblance to the police mugshot that was almost certainly being used to frighten the public. Women loved his blue eyes: many had told him so, and he'd taken advantage of it. "You're being most helpful, but I need to see her face to face. Can you tell me where she is?"

Emily responded to his charm offensive. "I'll ring through to Dee Saxton's suite," she said.

"Thank you," Shaun said. Fearful that Dee would somehow know it was not Marshall, and the lie would be uncovered, he nevertheless spoke with confidence. Realising his hands were trembling, he concentrated on steadying them.

Emily removed a phone from an oversized cream clutch bag. "Dee, it's Emily. How's it going?" She paused. "I beg your pardon, Jackie. I have a gentleman to see Kat White. Can she speak on the phone?"

"I'd like to see her personally," Shaun said.

"He wishes to see her personally," Emily echoed. "It's Mr Marshall Jenner. Will that be possible?" She waited for a reply. Evidently, it was affirmative, for she then said, "Thank you. I'll send him up then." She replaced the handset.

"Good news," she told Shaun. "The ladies are having their make-up done. They requested that you join them for a glass of champagne when they're finished, but please don't take photos of the bride's dress. They don't want the groom to see it before the wedding."

"No photos," Shaun said. "Scout's honour. I'll go there now, shall I?" He kept his smile respectful rather than triumphant.

152

"They need a while longer," Emily said. "Have a coffee in the lounge." She gestured to the velvet sofas. "My treat. Let's give them ten minutes."

"Make it an Irish coffee, and you're on," Shaun said, replacing his sunglasses.

Chapter 41.   Kat

Kat was admiring the stunning view of the London Eye when she heard the click of stilettos rising on the stairs. Finally, Dee was emerging from the bedroom of her split-level suite.

"The big reveal," Dee said, entering the living room. "What do you think, Kat?"

"You look sensational," Kat said, lounging on a velvet chair, a flute of champagne by her side. All that stopped her drinking it was the presence of a make-up artist adding scarlet gel nails to each finger.

Kat meant every word. Dee and her bridesmaids could have starred in a Hollywood movie. Their skin looked air-brushed, their glossy hair tonged into romantic ringlets.

The bride wore a dress of palest blush pink silk, sleeveless, slim-fitting and filmy. Sewn with pearls and butterflies in the same colour, it set off her shapely figure to perfection. Her bridesmaids' gowns took the same simple shape, but in co-ordinating shades without any adornment. Jackie, Dee's schoolfriend, was a blonde bombshell in a bubblegum colour. Auburn-haired Amy had chosen peach.

"We're all goddesses today," Amy said.

Jackie giggled. "And George is a god."

Dee's young toddler, George, was optimistically clad in white shirt, cream waistcoat and bow tie. Jackie was feeding him Milky Bar buttons in the hope that the marks wouldn't show.

A photographer, suited and bearded, bounded up the steps behind Dee. "A few photos, ladies," he demanded, snapping away.

Chocolate finished, Dee's little god smeared a hand over his black trousers. "Want Daddy," he complained.

Kat wondered if she was ready for motherhood. While the other women were cooing over George, she couldn't understand how they found a small child so interesting.

Dee sponged the little boy's hand and clothes with a baby wipe. "Perhaps Chas would like to entertain him for a bit," she said with a grin.

"I'll take him," Amy said.

"And I'll come with you," Jackie said. "We'll check that the groom has turned up."

For a moment, the light in Dee's eyes dimmed.

"Just joking," Jackie said. "Of course he'll turn up. George doesn't really need to see him before the wedding, anyway. Amy and I can take him for a walk around the hotel. There's a lovely heated terrace downstairs." She tickled the toddler under his armpits. "You want to explore, don't you, Georgie?"

George's laughter bubbled like a waterfall. "Yes," he lisped.

"I'll come with you," the photographer said. "I've got to set up in the River Room."

"We'll be back in twenty," Amy called, as they descended the staircase to the front door of the suite. Carved out of a tower at the top of the building, it was like a separate, upside-down flat. There was a sumptuous ensuite bedroom downstairs, where Dee had made herself ready, and a circular living room with views all over London on the top floor.

"Amy's usually so self-conscious," Kat said. "I'm surprised she's letting the public see her in that dress."

"Doesn't she look amazing?" Dee said. "You've done a great job on all of us, Tiffany."

The young make-up artist, a slim black girl with Afro hair, ripped jeans and velvet T-shirt, beamed. "Glad you like it, Dee." She gently removed Kat's hands from the UV lamp that dried the nails. "There. Finishing touches done."

"You can drink your fizz now, Kat," Dee said.

Kat shuddered. "I can't face it, I'm afraid," she admitted. "I poured it without thinking. Old habits die hard."

"I'll take it," Tiffany said.

"Why not?" Dee said. "Your work is done for the day. In fact, go home with one of those." She pointed to the coffee table, where a vast chrome bowl was filled with ice and bottles of Taittinger. "Are you all right, Kat?"

A telephone rang just as Tiffany left, and Kat was on the point of explaining she was pregnant.

"Hello?" Dee said, taking a call on the desk phone that sat on a polished black console table. "Yes, send him up." She turned to Kat. "Marshall Jenner wants to see us before the wedding, according to the concierge. Jackie mentioned it about an hour ago. I can't think what he wants."

"He's the MP, isn't he?" Kat was digging deep into her memory banks now. There had been a scandal. She could hardly recall any details. Coming from Bazakistan, she expected all politicians to be corrupt.

"An ex-MP. He's married to one of my dear friends, Jeannie." Dee frowned. "Between you and me, she's getting fed up with him, and rightly so. He's been flaunting his toy boys all over London."

"He's gay?" Kat was starting to remember. Marshall Jenner's downfall had involved both love and money, making his disgrace especially newsworthy.

"Yes," Dee said. "Jeannie deserves better. She's a charming lady." She whispered. "He's ugly, unemployed, and just wants her money. I bet he wants to tell me she's feeling stressed and isn't coming to the wedding, after all. That would be a shame."

Kat did her best to look sympathetic. "Why doesn't she kick him out?" she asked.

"You've hit the nail on the head," Dee said. "That's exactly what she should do. I was hoping to introduce her to my brother today. He's been single since his marriage broke up, and he's down on his luck. Jeannie would be good for him. She's got both beauty and banknotes."

"And brains?" Kat asked.

"I doubt it," Dee said. "Her marriage speaks for itself. But Davey wouldn't expect brains, because no one's as clever as him. I always struggled at school, while he came top at everything. He was more intelligent than me and all our friends."

Ross was too, Kat thought. Her former fiancé was arrogant with it, but perhaps Dee's brother wasn't.

"I just thought," Dee mused, "it would be fun to do some matchmaking today. I'd like to start off a romance or two, otherwise the party will end up being all about business networking."

"I thought guests came to a wedding for a good time," Kat said.

"Of course. But for some of my friends, that's their idea of a good time. I often organise networking events, and I'm sure a few deals will be done after the ceremony. As you say, old habits die hard. So I'd like them to meet interesting people. It was why I invited your boss, Marty."

"He's not my boss," Kat interjected. "He's my business partner." It might be an unequal relationship, but she didn't defer to Marty if she could avoid it.

"He's Amy's boss, though, isn't he?" Dee said. "Anyway, Chas insisted I invite you, so I decided it would be nice for you if Marty was there as well."

How little Dee knew of her, Kat reflected. "So Charles insisted, did he?"

"He felt you brought us together," Dee said. "For that reason alone, he didn't need to insist. You've always been top of my guest list." She gave Kat a warm hug.

The suite's doorbell sounded.

"That'll be Marshall," Dee said. She put a finger to her lips. "Not a word, please, Kat."

"You can rely on me," Kat said. "I'll open the door."

She went downstairs to do so. Whatever she expected, it wasn't the man who stood before her – the killer who had followed her to Birmingham three years before, believing wrongly that she'd stolen twenty thousand pounds from his casino.

"Hello, Kat," Shaun Halloran said, his blue eyes brimming with hatred and devoid of reason.

She opened her mouth to scream.

"I'll give you something to shout about," Shaun said. He punched the side of her head, hard, sending her reeling.

Chapter 42. Shaun

Power coursed through Shaun's body as Kat staggered backwards. He must press home his advantage while she was still in shock. "Don't make a sound, or there will be more of that," he threatened her.

Kat was as beautiful as he remembered. Everything about her oozed class: her blonde hair, curled for the wedding, her creamy skin, the glossy nails that matched her red cocktail dress.

He closed the door behind him, then slowly ran his gaze over that hourglass figure, taking in his surroundings at the same time. They were inside a small, square lobby, with another door ahead of him and stairs leading upwards.

"Let's talk privately. Just you and me," he said. "Where's the bedroom?"

He saw fear rise like a flame in her eyes. It fed his energy. For the first time, he understood how rapists took such pleasure in their crimes. It wasn't so much the act itself, enjoyable though it was, but the total control over their victim's mind and body. As Shaun's libido rose, his resolve hardened. Whatever the temptation, she wasn't going to turn him into a nonce. They were beneath contempt. He didn't see why he shouldn't frighten her before pulling the trigger, though.

A woman yelled from the top of the stairs. "What's happening, Kat? Send him up." He recognised Dee's voice.

The plum returned to Shaun's mouth. "In a second, darling," he called. He hissed at Kat, "Who else is here?"

"The photographer and his assistant. They're kickboxers," she said.

She was bluffing, surely? "Hellooo," he called, in those stupidly cultured tones.

"Hello," Dee echoed.

"Just you and delicious Dee," Shaun said. "Why is it with you that I always get two birds for the price of one? First, your friend Amy protects you when you lead me a merry dance through the middle of England. Now it's the luscious bride-to-be." He leered, all the better to terrify her. "Where's the bedroom? Upstairs?" He gripped her arm.

Kat twisted from his grasp. Flipping from sullen compliance to vengeful fury, she launched a knee at his groin. Her hands clawed at his eyes.

Taken by surprise, Shaun dodged her red talons, which simply raked his cheeks. He wasn't so lucky with the knee. Recoiling at the explosion of pain within him, he fought back, thumping her savagely. All his weight was channelled into his fists as he landed blows to Kat's stomach and the soft tissues below.

It was an instinctive reaction. He'd never hit his wife, or other females among his family, friends and employees. The taboo didn't apply to Kat, the woman whose evidence had sent him inside. He dragged the gun from his pocket. "Now, do as you're told."

Doubled up in pain, Kat still wouldn't surrender. "No way," she said, spitting out the words even as tears flowed from her green eyes.

"What's going on?" Dee, her tone inquisitive but still polite and confident, descended the staircase in her bridal gown. She was even more stunning than she'd appeared on television.

Shaun froze, recalling Meg on their wedding day, slim and beautiful. He blinked the thought away.

Dee stopped halfway down the stairs, her enquiring expression faltering at the sight before her. "You're not Marshall," she said.

"You don't say," Shaun replied. He pointed the pistol at Dee. "Kat, you wouldn't ruin the party, would you? All those shiny, happy people are waiting for the bride. She won't be there if she's dead."

Dee clung to the banister. She appeared on the verge of fainting.

"I'll kill Dee if you don't behave, Kat." Shaun glared at his adversary. "Understand?"

Kat nodded. She was pale, her face tear-streaked and seemingly in agony.

Shaun felt smug. At last, she knew who was boss. "Come downstairs," he told Dee, "and into that room." He pointed to the door behind Kat. "Kat is going to tie you up. Because you won't die if she behaves. This is between her and me."

He licked his lips. "I was going to give you a quick death," he said, "but you've spoiled it for yourself. I'll be taking my time."

An old-fashioned Nokia ringtone suddenly cut through the air. It took Shaun a few seconds to realise it was his phone. He ignored it. His prize was within his grasp. Everything else could wait.

Chapter 43.　　Ben

Successful gaming was all about strategic thinking. You had to be in control, staying at least two steps ahead of your opponents. This time, everything had changed. The enemy was Ben's father, and he was out of control.

Ben's face was strained as he parked in front of the hotel. He should have known better. Having seen the old man's sanity crumble a little further at every visit, he'd persuaded himself to rescue his father from prison. He'd never expected murder to form part of the package. What had he unleashed?

At least, as Vince had said, it hadn't taken Ben long to discover where his father had gone. Kat was attending a society wedding in a swish hotel by the Thames. It was three stops from Fitzrovia on the tube, by far the quickest means of travel.

Once he reached the surface at Embankment tube station, Ben checked both his mobiles. Vince and Shaun were only supposed to call the cheap, disposable phone, but he knew his father, for one, had the other number. There were no messages for him. He tried to ring Shaun for the third time in an hour. As before, the call went straight to voicemail. Ben scuttled out of the station and found a deserted corner under a railway arch. He spoke briefly, saying a passport in the name of Colin Shanahan was available and the flight had been rearranged. However, if anyone was killed, he was cancelling the plane and calling the police.

Ben followed this with a text message to the same effect. His patience was about to snap. He told himself there could be an alternative explanation. His father might have lost his phone or been recaptured. It was still the old man's own fault: as usual, Shaun was doing exactly what he wanted and leaving everyone else to sweep up the mess.

He found the building, and hesitated before entering. Until now, his actions in helping Shaun escape had been untraceable. By looking for his father in the hotel, he risked detection. He wondered if Shaun's freedom, or Kat's life, were worth it. Tempted to turn around, he noticed muffled banging and whimpering noises from the boot of a car parked nearby. What was in there? It sounded like a dog. A pang of sympathy overwhelmed him, propelling him forward. A stranger's life, or an animal's well-being, meant nothing within the fantasy of a video game. In the real world, they were worth fighting for.

"Will you call the RSPCA, please? There's a dog locked in that Merc's boot," he said to the hotel doorman.

The man didn't open the door for him. "Good morning, Sir. Can I help you?" he asked.

Ben guessed it was his jeans and parka that were causing concern. While he hadn't been here before, he'd stayed in other five-star hotels for gaming conventions, or had drinks with journalists. Perhaps this one didn't see many gamers; they tended to be more casually dressed than other guests.

"I'm meeting a journalist," he lied. "Like I said, please can you call the RSPCA?"

Inside the hotel, a dozen men in suits had arrived at the concierge's desk before him. Wearing prominent name-badges, they were obviously delegates at a business conference. Ben listened casually to their conversation, then tuned out as he realised it related to new accountancy rules.

Of more interest were a trio standing nearby. It was the pretty young redhead who first caught his eye. At first, he thought she was a guest at the wedding, the daughter of the middle-aged couple with her.

He adjusted his thoughts on closer scrutiny. The girl was in business attire, a crimson trouser suit, while her elders were more flamboyant: a black suit and brocade waistcoat for him, a fuchsia satin dress for her.

"You've come for Charles Satterthwaite and Dee Saxton's wedding, I assume?" the girl said.

"That's right," the man said. "Marshall and Jeannie Jenner."

"Hi, I'm Alice," the girl said, shaking each of their hands in turn. She looked at an iPad. "This says you're already here. Did you see my colleague, Emily?"

"We've only just come down from our room," the man said. "You wouldn't believe how long it takes Jeannie to get ready."

"That's strange. Marshall Jenner has been ticked off the list," Alice replied.

"I can assure you, this really is Marshall Jenner," his partner said, "and I should know, because I'm his wife." Her bright dress and extreme thinness gave her the appearance of a stick of rock.

161

"I'm surprised you don't recognise me," the man said. "I'm infamous."

His companion giggled, then busied her fingers tucking stray tendrils of dyed blonde hair into a jewel-encrusted bun. "Marshall's a legend," she said.

"Is my wife on your list?" the man asked. "Jeannie Jenner."

Alice smiled. "Yes, she's on the list with no tick as yet," she said. "Hang on, I see Emily left a comment. She took you – I mean Marshall Jenner – to the Tower Suite, to see Kat White."

"Who's Kat White?" Jeannie asked, looking unamused.

"I don't know," Marshall said.

Ben didn't wait to hear more. He dashed to the bank of lifts signposted from the lobby. The Tower Suite would be at the top of the building, wouldn't it? He was sure he knew who had been taken to see Kat. If he didn't act fast, she'd be dead.

Chapter 44.   Kat

Agony shot through Kat's abdomen: a twinge like a red-hot knife. She opened her mouth to groan, but no sound emerged. Instead, the nausea that had gripped her constantly for three months reached a crescendo. She vomited: over the scarlet dress, the velvety carpet, and Shaun's shoes. He jumped backwards, cursing.

For a second or two, his focus shifted from the weapon in his hand. The distraction was enough for Dee, two steps above the foot of the stairs, to spring towards him. She grabbed Shaun like a koala curling around a tree: her arms grasping his neck, her legs encircling his body. The wedding dress gathered in silky folds around her bottom.

Kat heard Dee say something about a gun. The comment was loud, conveying urgency, but hardly making sense. She was dizzy with the shock and pain of Shaun's attack.

What was happening to the baby? She hadn't wanted the child, but that was no reason to let Shaun murder it. If he took her life, the baby wouldn't survive. She retched, suspecting to her horror that his onslaught had already killed the child. Why else was a cramp twisting its way through her belly?

They were all going to die, even Dee, despite her bravery. Shaun was a ruthless killer, after all. Somehow, Kat had to stop him. She staggered against his right arm, hoping he'd drop the pistol.

He flailed upwards, pushing her away, doubtless intending to shoot her but unable to control the gun properly. Dee had seen to that. Her face was in Shaun's, screaming at him, biting him and obscuring his vision.

The gun connected with Kat's nose, the violence of the blow so great that she lost her balance.

Shaun's phone rang again, then stopped. Someone banged on the other side of the door to the suite. "Let me in," a man's voice yelled.

Shaun thrashed around, his left hand managing to unlatch the door. "Help me, son," he gasped. "Get rid of these crazy bitches."

Shaun's son? She was as good as dead already, Kat thought, noting the floppy brown fringe and treacherous blue eyes of the not-quite stranger as the room began to spin.

Chapter 45.   Ben

Ben gagged on the stench of vomit and blood. For a frozen moment, he took in the bizarre scene. His father, a gun in his hand, was grappling with a blonde in a wedding dress. Kat lay still on the floor. A trickle of blood, its colour matching her scarlet outfit, snaked across her face. He was too late. His father had murdered her.

Fear, rage and despair gripped him. He howled, an inarticulate animal sound that gradually formed into words. "Why, Dad? Why?"

"Kill them," Shaun roared. "Take my gun."

The door was barely open. Ben pushed, and the rest of his body followed his head through the gap.

"Take my gun," his father repeated, his left arm thrashing out and landing a punch on his opponent's kidneys. She was entangled around him, clenching him like a vice.

The blonde screamed in pain, her legs losing their grip. She bit Shaun's nose and attempted to strangle him.

"Bitch," Shaun snarled, fishing a six-inch knife from his pocket and plunging it into her back.

Darting in front of them and picking his way over Kat's prone body, Ben grabbed the pistol. "Stop," he shouted. "Both of you."

The firearm felt heavy, nothing like a video game controller or the plastic toys he recalled from his childhood. He knew what to do with it, though: point and shoot. Was it loaded? His father certainly thought so, although he'd clearly been using it already.

Ben glanced at Kat, wishing he'd arrived a minute earlier. Bile caught in his throat. He forced himself to stay calm. No one could bring her back from the dead, but he could save her friend.

The blonde's screams rose in pitch and intensity. A bloodstain spread around the knife's hilt.

Shaun swore. "Get on with it, Ben," he demanded, trying to push the blonde away.

"I'll shoot both of you if you don't stop fighting," Ben said, amazed at how confidently the words emerged. He edged backwards up the stairs, training the gun on both combatants.

His father stood stock still, his mouth shocked. The woman unpeeled herself from Shaun, stumbling and almost tripping over Kat's body.

164

"Call an ambulance," she shrieked, sobbing. "Please. He's stabbed me. Look," she pointed to Kat, "this girl's hurt too."

Kat needed an undertaker, not an ambulance. If Ben didn't get help soon, the blonde would join her. He didn't dare remove the knife from her back, despite the red circle growing around it.

He glared at his father. "I tried to tell you, but you wouldn't listen. No more killing."

Fury consumed his father's eyes, the mad gaze of a monster in a video game. "You're crazy," Shaun said, flinging himself towards the staircase, pinning Ben to the steps as he tried to seize the pistol.

When you fought a boss on a screen, you didn't smell blood, sweat and the hot, sour breath of a smoker. Ben gagged.

Any second now, Shaun would win the pistol.

"I love you, Dad, but it has to stop," Ben said. He pulled the trigger, feeling the pistol recoil into his hand, hearing the boom of the bullet tearing into his father's flesh.

The rage left Shaun Halloran's eyes. They blinked. The hand that had reached for the gun twitched once, and was still. The bloodied corpse of Ben's father toppled onto him.

Ben howled. What had he done?

As if animated by a ghost, Kat's body stirred.

Chapter 46.   Marty

"You look like a waiter," Marty told Charles.

Amy's father laughed. "I was afraid you'd say that. A rather superior waiter, I hope? Dee persuaded me into this ridiculous get-up against my better judgement. Everything must be colour co-ordinated for her big day."

Charles was wearing a cream suit and bow tie, as were his ushers and best man. While Marty would have burst out of the tight brocade waistcoat, the groom was slim and dapper. He had an annoyingly full head of dark hair too.

A genuine waiter hovered nearby with a tray of champagne glasses. Charles took two, handing one to Marty. "Bottoms up!"

"This is very generous," Marty said. "At most weddings, you're lucky to have a thimbleful of cava once the knot's been tied. I've never had a drink beforehand without taking myself off to the pub."

Charles grinned, swigging most of his fizz. "Personally, I think it's a great idea. It helps to relieve the stress. Really, it's Dee's way of making sure her friends have a good time. She's an avid networker and she imagines everyone else is the same."

"Is that why there are so many guests?"

Charles looked around the gracious room, lavishly decorated with marble columns and a richly painted ceiling. It was buzzing with conversation, oiled by copious quantities of champagne.

"This is nothing," he said. "After the wedding breakfast, we're expecting another two hundred for the reception. Drinks, dancing, a tribute band; the full works. For now, it's just close friends and family."

"We're privileged, then." Angela appeared at Marty's elbow.

"May I introduce my wife, Angela?" Marty said. He looked her up and down. "Your visit to the powder room's paid off, bab. You're twenty-one again."

Angela, slinky in a skin-tight silver dress, a diamanté tiara adorning her short golden curls, held out her right hand. "Charmed to meet you, Charles. Thanks for inviting us. I've heard so much about your wedding from Amy. She's really excited about it."

"Me too," Charles said.

"I saw your intended on TV earlier," Angela said. "I'm a great fan of hers."

"Angela's got all her DVDs," Marty said.

"She didn't look nervous at all. Not a butterfly," Angela said. "How about you? Have you got your speech ready for later?"

"I'm going to keep it short," Charles said. "I'll have had plenty of Dutch courage first." He tapped his glass.

Several heads turned at the ringing sound.

"False alarm," Charles told them. "The registrar isn't here yet." He winced. "My biggest fear, Angela, is that George will lose the rings. He's bringing them down the aisle on a cushion. It's a big responsibility for a two-year-old."

Marty wondered why Charles had agreed to it. He supposed Dee called the shots.

"Two is such a sweet age," Angela gushed. "Look at him, over there with Amy. She's pretty as a picture, Charles. You must be proud."

"Very."

At the other end of the long room, Amy was standing hand in hand with George. Copper ringlets tumbled onto the shoulders of her simple peach sheath. Her face glowed.

Erik, chatting with Tim nearby, was gazing at his girlfriend with wide eyes.

Angela nudged Marty in the ribs. "I bet they'll be next. When Dee throws her bouquet, you wait and see who catches it."

"Amy scrubs up well," Marty agreed.

George slipped out of Amy's grasp and ran to Charles, neatly evading two dozen pairs of legs on the way. "Daddy," the little boy gasped.

"Georgie," Charles said, lifting the child into his arms and pointing him at a large window. "Look outside at the big river." There was a spectacular view of the Thames. Pleasure boats were sailing past, and the London Eye dominated the skyline.

A girl in a red suit, one of the wedding planners, approached them. "The registrar's here, Charles."

"Do excuse me," Charles said. "I'm needed elsewhere. Not long now."

Angela held out her arms. "Lend him to me, Charles."

George was perfectly willing to be passed to her.

"Look at the boats," Angela said.

"Boat," George repeated. "Want one."

Amy saved the day, whisking George away for ring duty. They vanished after Charles.

The red-suited girl returned, shepherding them to a smaller adjacent function room. Chairs were arranged theatre-style, their focus on an ornate oak fireplace festooned with cream silk roses. Similar floral decorations were pinned to the curtains, hanging from chandeliers and scattered across a table in front of the fireplace.

Here, Charles fidgeted in one of the grey plush chairs, an empty place beside him. The registrar, a fiftyish woman neat in a dark bob and navy jacket, sat opposite.

Marty and Angela were directed to sit near the back. The front row was reserved for George, the bridesmaids and the best man. Immediately behind them, Dee and Charles' parents sat with their other children and grandchildren.

Tim remained on his feet, making a beeline for Marty. "Did Amy say where Kat was?" he asked.

"No. Didn't you arrive together?"

"She went ahead to see the bridesmaids. I was supposed to meet her ten minutes ago."

"Amy didn't say anything. Kat's probably trowelling on more slap. Have you tried phoning her?"

"She's not answering," Tim said. Worry lines creased his otherwise handsome features.

The wedding planner gestured to a seat.

"Sorry, Alice, I'm still waiting for my girlfriend." A true salesman, he'd remembered the young woman's name.

"It isn't Kat White, is it? Emily took her to the Tower Suite, I think," Alice said. "I'll call her."

A bearded photographer stood in a corner of the room, video camera trained on the door. The minutes ticked past. Kat didn't appear. Nor did Dee, George or the bridesmaids. The photographer looked at his watch. Alice spoke briefly with Charles before leaving the room.

Two fifteen approached, then two thirty. The tension in the air was palpable. Tim paced up and down. Charles's shoulders were hunched. The happy chatter of the guests had ceased, as silence prevailed. Was Dee doing a runner?

The door swung open, heralding Alice's return. She was accompanied by an armed policeman. They whispered to Charles.

The groom rose to his feet to address the guests. "I'm sorry. We have to postpone the wedding. There's been an incident, and Dee is on her way to hospital. The hotel is in lockdown. Please can you all stay where you are."

"Any news of Kat?" Tim's face was pale.

"She's going to hospital too," Alice said, concern filling her eyes.

Chapter 47.   Kat

"Kat, Kat!"

Who could it be? It was a male voice she didn't recognise. A bright light was shining in her eyes.

"She's with us," the same voice said.

Kat blinked. The light receded. Stars danced before her eyes, then she saw the man in the hi-vis jacket. He was holding a torch.

She tried to sit up. Her body felt heavy, as if she couldn't breathe. When she moved, pain raced from her belly to her head.

"What happened?" She'd barely whispered the words when too many memories came flooding back.

"You've had a shock. I'm taking you to hospital to check you over. Your friend's gone there already."

A policeman loomed like a black and chequered skyscraper above them. "We need to question this one."

"You'll have to do it later," hi-vis man, obviously a paramedic, said. "Send one of your team in the ambulance with her."

A cramp did a devil dance through Kat's abdomen. She screamed. "My baby!"

"Hush," hi-vis man said. "We mustn't jump to conclusions. We need to get you to hospital. If we can save your baby, we will."

It had to be a miscarriage. She'd never felt so ill in her life. Nor had her spirit ever been so crushed. Kat whimpered, keening to herself.

"Let me in!" Erik was shouting somewhere in the distance.

"I want to see my girlfriend." Tim's voice was even louder.

There were sounds of a discussion. "Back off. You're not allowed in there."

That was a small relief. Kat couldn't bear to see Tim. How could she look into his eyes, and tell him his dreams of fatherhood were over? She was flaky, treacherous and worthless; she'd attracted a murderer to her child.

"Shaun?" she asked, guessing and hoping that the police presence was bad news for him.

"Is that the older man's name?" the paramedic asked the policeman.

"Yes."

"He's dead. His son called the emergency services, but there was nothing we could do for him."

At least she was free of Shaun Halloran, but at a price that was far too high. She tasted salt, and realised it was her tears.

Chapter 48. Vince

Having been up at stupid o'clock, hared to Broxbourne and back, and pulled strings to secure Shaun's passport, Vince was exhausted. There was no speed, coke or even coffee in his flat, and he couldn't be bothered to go out to get any. He went back to bed.

The constant hum of traffic on the High Road didn't disturb him. He expected his wake-up call would be the ringing of his phone once Ben had found his father. Instead, it was an insistent knocking at his door.

"Open up! Police."

They must have found Shaun again. Vince rubbed his eyes, and threw off his duvet. It was still light outside. He was dressed in the jeans, white shirt and black cotton waistcoat he'd been wearing that morning.

The knocking became a pounding. The lawmen were putting some heft into it: the wooden door was beginning to splinter near the hinges. Vince stuffed his phones and wallet in his jeans pocket, and considered his options. His studio flat had no fire escape. Its only window was a Velux giving onto the roof, and he didn't rate his chances of abseiling down the four-storey building. His eyes lit upon the loft hatch above his bed. Although the tiny apartment was a converted attic, the apex of the roof remained an unused void. Vince remembered Shaun, who boasted of breaking into a hundred houses by the age of sixteen, telling him that burglars never bothered with lofts. Perhaps the filth didn't either.

There was no time even to hide the three cannabis plants on a shelf below the Velux. Swiftly, Vince punched the square hatch upwards and to one side, then pulled himself into the cavity above. He replaced the hatch, crouching on the wooden framework around it, just as the door below crunched open.

Gradually, Vince's eyes adjusted to the space around him. It wasn't pitch-black, as he'd expected. Chinks of daylight emerged between the roof tiles. At their highest point, he could kneel, but couldn't stand. The floor was covered with fluffy insulation material, topped with a layer of dust. This dispersed in a cloud as Vince prodded it, hoping to find boards underneath. There were none, simply a lattice of wooden joists a couple of feet apart. He balanced on one of them, stifling a sneeze as dust assailed his nostrils.

Below, he heard the police, a man and a woman, talking as they searched the flat.

"The bed's still warm, Kyle. Will you check the wardrobe?"

"Scared to look at his manhood, Nat? He's no use to you; he bats for the other side."

They established quickly enough that Vince wasn't in the studio.

"He can't have got far, Nat," the man said. "We'll get him sooner or later."

"Everyone else is in custody," she said. "Jonathan Halloran's already inside."

Vince jolted upright at the mention of Jon's name, almost falling off the timber support. Horrified, he continued to listen.

Kyle laughed. "Those woodentops in Hertfordshire must have had a shock when the family dog turned up with a human bone. Goodness knows what they thought they had on their hands: a witches' coven, or some such."

"They were investigating a holiday scam, weren't they?" Nat said.

"Something like that," Kyle said. "The vegan who said she was made ill by a chicken curry. You couldn't make it up."

"I blame the lawyers," she said. "I was cold-called today and asked if I'd been on holiday. They said I could make a food poisoning claim if I had."

"I bet you told them to get lost, didn't you?" Kyle said. "Next time, get their number and report it." He sighed. "Let's go. I suppose we have to try that address in West Ham next. It's been a good day, though. Enough information to give one Halloran a life sentence, and another one dead."

"Shaun, the dead man, is the father, isn't he?" Nat said, as Vince was puzzling over Kyle's last remark.

A sudden gust of wind outside rattled through the roof tiles, whipping up the dust. As it filled Vince's mouth and nose, he struggled to breath. His cough and sneeze were instinctive. Caught unawares, his body jerked; enough to topple him from his precarious perch. One of his legs crashed through the flimsy plasterboard of the studio's ceiling.

"What have we here?" Kyle asked, his voice heavy with irony.

173

Chapter 49.   Kat

It was Kat's first day back at the distillery. Thick make-up covered her bruises. Her heart would take longer to heal. Still, she told herself, she was lucky: Dee, while recovering, remained in hospital.

No longer pregnant, the only answer to the maelstrom of emotions swirling within her was to throw herself into her work.

Marty called within the first hour. "How are you getting on?" he asked, his voice uncharacteristically gentle.

"Fine," Kat said. "No sudden crises erupted in my absence." She'd only been away for a week.

"Glad to hear it," he said. "I'd never be able to let you take a holiday otherwise. Listen, I've been investigating new factory units for you. There are a couple up for auction. Can you come over later to discuss your needs, please?"

How typical of Marty to look at auction properties. He wouldn't knowingly overpay for anything.

"Is Tim there?" she asked.

"No, he's on the road."

That was a relief. "I can be there at three," she said.

She'd avoided Tim since the miscarriage. An unfamiliar, and devastating, sensation of guilt overwhelmed her. He'd trusted her to carry his child, and she'd failed him. She could never atone for that.

Kat busied herself until the last minute, lighting a cigarette the second she was outside the building. She'd turned to nicotine for emotional support. Tempted though she was to smoke in the distillery, she wasn't about to risk an explosion.

A gold Subaru was parked in the street. Kat turned on her heel and marched away. She hoped he'd think she hadn't seen him.

She heard footsteps. "Hello, stranger."

"Tim." She couldn't ignore him any longer. With a deep breath, she spun around and looked into his blue eyes. "I'm sorry."

"You've got nothing to apologise for."

"I brought it on myself – on the baby. If I hadn't chased easy money to work for Shaun all those years ago, none of this would have happened." She began to cry.

"Don't. Kat, you mustn't blame yourself. That's the road to madness. He was a psychopath." Tim kissed her lips.

The familiar desire surged through her.

"I don't want to stop doing this, but I have to," Tim said. "I've got a question I should have asked you months ago, but I was too chicken. Will you marry me, Kat?"

She stared at him, so astonished that the flow of tears stemmed. "I thought you'd never ask."

"And I was afraid you'd never say yes," Tim said.

Caution held her back. "Is it because of the baby – because you feel sorry for me?"

Tim shook his head, his eyes pleading. "No, although I sympathise, without a doubt. I'm asking because I love you and I want to spend my life with you. So, what's your answer?"

Chapter 50.   Ben

The funeral had taken place in Wanstead, in a Roman Catholic church to which the Halloran clan returned like homing pigeons on high days and holidays. Ben had paid for a wake afterwards, but didn't attend, deterred by glares and hisses from his cousins during the requiem mass. That didn't sting as much as his brother's reaction. Jon, shackled between two prison officers, had refused to speak to him.

Instead, Ben drove to the White Horse, a pub he knew his father had enjoyed visiting in happier times, and drank a pint of lager in remembrance. Then, realising from the regulars' stares that he was recognised, he left. In the pub's car park, he found all of the GTi's tyres were flat. They'd been punctured with nails.

He arranged for a breakdown truck to tow the car to a garage, then took an Uber to his favourite café in Hackney. He'd lost the appetite for shoot'em ups, but escaping into a fantasy game took his mind off the past again. He didn't even notice Kyle Lassiter's arrival.

"Hello, Ben."

He looked up to see the policeman, wearing jeans and hoodie like half the café's patrons. Out of uniform, Lassiter still displayed the self-importance of the prefect in the playground.

"Plainclothes visit, is it, Kyle?"

Lassiter coughed. "I'm off duty," he said. His features formed themselves into a semblance of sympathy. "I'm sorry about your dad. I know you tried to get him to give himself up."

"It's history," Ben said. "I'm glad it's over."

It wasn't over, of course, although the police had eventually accepted his version of events. He'd been arrested on suspicion of murder, but then it turned out that Dee had spoken up for him.

No one could prove he was involved in his father's escape, either, and he wasn't telling Lassiter. Nor would he speak about the guilt, sorrow, fear and relief that churned in his mind when he wasn't gaming. During his schooldays, he'd learned not to let emotions show.

"I just wondered," Lassiter said. "My kid brother loves these games. He'd like to get into eSports. Would you talk to him about it?"

"All right," Ben said. "Send him into the café. I spend time here most days, unless I'm away at a tournament."

"I'll tell him," Lassiter said. "Thanks. I just thought it would keep him on the straight and narrow."

"Okay," Ben said, reluctant to prolong the conversation. "I'm starting another game in a second. I'll see you around."

He guessed he'd had as much of an apology as he was ever going to get.

Chapter 51.   Marty

"Another day, another beer," Marty said, kicking off his shoes and heading for the kitchen. "What's for dinner, Angela?"

Her voice carried from the floor above. "I thought we could go out. In fact, I've booked a table."

"I'll go anywhere that's not a salad bar," he called to her, helping himself to a bottle of Two Towers Birmingham Mild. If she jibbed at the calorie count, he'd tell her it was full of vitamins.

Angela appeared, clad in the same silver dress she'd worn to the wedding that didn't happen. She must have received compliments for it. It hadn't stopped her buying a new one, hanging in the wardrobe to wear when Charles and Dee finally rescheduled.

"Tim tells me you've got lots to celebrate," she said.

"Yes, there's money in the bank, Erik's cancer research is back on, and I've got outline planning permission for Florence Street."

His elderly warehouse would be replaced by shiny student flats. He wouldn't be sorry to leave. The story of Hajji and Hero Couriers across the road was beginning to unfold in a criminal court: a fantastical tale of four jihadi terrorists and a police sting.

"And there's more," Angela said. "I hear you've got a major supermarket deal for Starshine vodka."

"You're well-informed," Marty said.

Angela smiled. "I had a cup of tea with Kat and Tim. Aren't they besotted with each other? What a lovely young couple."

Marty winced. "I wouldn't go that far," he said. "At least, for half of the duo."

"Kat's pretty, though, isn't she?" Angela teased. "You know," she added, "Tim said the Starshine deal was all down to her."

"It was," Marty admitted. "Those supermarket buyers aren't easy people to deal with, and she ran rings round them."

He'd been impressed by Kat's negotiating skills and energy. Her new distillery was up and running too. Buying a factory at auction, he'd completed on the purchase quickly, securing a bank loan with no fuss once Ray saw the order book. Kat had been equally swift to acquire equipment and staff. She was producing ten times as much vodka as before. When she set her mind to it, she could achieve great results.

"I like her," Angela stated, baldly. "She went through hell, but she's bouncing back. She always does. You see her as a gold-digger sinking her hooks into Tim, but suppose it's the other way round? Kat could be a goldmine for you."

His wife was right, of course, but if he told her, she'd be unbearably smug. Marty kept quiet.

"Anyway," Angela said, "Tim and Kat don't have much money, so I've offered them a marquee in our garden for their wedding."

Marty admitted defeat. "Fine," he said. "As long as there's Starshine vodka, and beer to drink, I'm happy." He sidled to the fridge for a second bottle. It was time to start practising.

THANK YOU

Thank you for reading **The Revenge Trail** - I hope you enjoyed it! I'd really appreciate it if you'd tell your friends by leaving a review on Amazon, Goodreads, or your blog.

I'd love to stay in touch with you, too. If you sign up for my newsletter at aaabbott.co.uk, I'll send you a free e-book of short stories. You'll also receive news about forthcoming books and live fiction events. I hope you can get to one; it would be wonderful to meet you.

You can also find me on Twitter (@AAAbbottStories) and Facebook.

Lightning Source UK Ltd.
Milton Keynes UK
UKHW041533010319
338177UK00001B/27/P